Hell with the Hide Off

Also published in Large Print from G.K. Hall by Jim Miller:

Rangers' Revenge
Shootout in Sendero

Hell with the Hide Off

Jim Miller

G.K. Hall & Co.
Thorndike, Maine

Published in Large Print by arrangement with Pocket Books, a division of Simon & Schuster Consumer Group, Inc.

G.K. Hall Large Print Book Series.

Printed on acid free paper in Great Britain.

The text of this Large Print edition is unabridged. Other aspects of the book may vary from the original edition.

Set in 16 Pt. Plantin.

Library of Congress Cataloging-in-Publication Data

Miller, Jim, 1945–
  Hell with the hide off / Jim Miller.
  p.   cm.
  ISBN 0-8161-5933-5 (alk. paper: lg. print)
  1. Large type books.   I. Title.
[PS3563.I4125H4   1994]   93–42948
813'.54—dc20   CIP

---

*This one's for
Diane, Sandy, Dot,
Dottie, GiGi, Val, and Janice.
They mean the world to me.*

CHAPTER ONE

Damn, but it was a shiny thing! Brand spanking new and shiny as could be, even without the sun glinting off of it. Still, I found myself going over it with my kerchief, as though I could make it shinier yet. Fact of the matter was, I was paying so much attention to it that I didn't hear the door open and my boys come in. Hell, the whole Comanche Nation could have paraded into my office about then and I do believe I'd never have known it!

'Well now, would you look at that,' Chance said, taking in the scene before him. When I didn't respond, he glanced at his brother. 'Looks like us about twenty years ago around Christmas time, wouldn't you say?'

'Wouldn't argue it for a minute,' Wash said, a grin as wide as his brother's coming to his face.

'All right,' I said, giving them my full attention as I hauled my git-up end off the edge of my desk and stood full upright. I'd had my head cocked enough to see the two once I knew they'd entered, taking in their moves and only half hearing their words. 'What is it you two birds want?'' When their smiles only widened, I added in a much

1

sterner voice, 'What's the matter, ain't you ever seen a man full of pride before?'

'Like I said, Wash,' Chance answered, looking at his brother with that smile, 'just like us at Christmas time.'

'You finally got it, huh, Pa?' Wash was ignoring his brother, and had a look of pride just like the one I was feeling my own self. Instead of some smart-alecky answer, he stuck out a paw and offered me congratulations. 'It's about time.'

I took his fist in both of mine and pumped it as though I were some proud new father who'd just taken on the responsibility of a child. Hell, that was the equivalent of how I was feeling at the moment. Not a bad comparison, if I do say so myself. I'd no doubt I was a mite flushed in the face too.

'That's a fact,' I said, still full of pride. 'Stage come through about ten this morning, an hour ago maybe. Had this tiny box for me.' I held up a small cardboard box no bigger than my fist. 'Had to sign for it and all. Real official like.'

'Let me see that thing,' Chance said. He took a step forward and thumbed the new badge I'd quickly stuck on my chest. His smile turned into a serious look for a moment, then he stuck out his paw and gave me a hardy handshake. 'Well, if anyone deserves to be a United States Deputy Marshal, I reckon you do, Pa.' I knew he

2

wasn't joshing me when he added, 'Wash is right. It's about time.'

'Ain't that the truth,' I said, more in comment to myself than anyone else. For one brief moment I recalled my career in law enforcement, if that's what you want to call it, and realized that it had been almost half my lifetime. It was Abel Ferris and me who had moved in and settled the town of Twin Rifles too many years ago to count. It was after I'd come back from the Mexican War that I'd taken to rangering with the Texas Rangers. When my boys had been old enough, I'd introduced each of them to the badge and responsibilities of being a ranger on the Texas frontier. I'd always thought that had been part of learning to be a man on this frontier for them. When the War Between the States had come along, I'd taken to wearing a badge for the town of Twin Rifles, especially when they disbanded the Texas Rangers.

It was reaching the fall of 1865 now, and the war hadn't quite been over six months yet, but I'd done a bit of politicking of my own with those in office to get an appointment as a federal lawman. Lord only knew we were needing more than our share of law and order hereabouts!

'Say,' I said, pulling my pocket watch out and giving it a quick glance, 'if this old ticker is still accurate, I'd gauge we can get us a

3

beer over at Johnson's saloon. What do you say?'

'Sounds good,' Chance said. Coffee, beer, or whiskey—I didn't know my oldest son to be one to turn down any of them if they were free.

'Besides,' Wash added, as we walked out the door, 'you can always open the saloon up a mite early if you've a mind to. Especially with that new badge.'

'Now don't let it get to your head like that, son,' I said in a serious manner, although in the back of my mind I wasn't sure that I couldn't do exactly what Wash was talking about if the need might occur. If this U.S. Marshal job was all it was cracked up to be, it carried some almighty powerful force with it, that much I knew for sure.

The saloon hadn't been open ten minutes when we arrived, so there wasn't much of a crowd gathered yet. It was just as well, for I never was much of a lavish spender. I dug into my pocket and produced a gold coin and put it on the bar and ordered drinks for the house, which included my boys and me and a couple of locals I immediately recognized.

I didn't have to do any bragging, for Chance and Wash seemed to be doing it for me, telling those who'd gather around how I'd just got appointed a U.S. Deputy Marshal to go along with my regular city

4

marshal job.

'Now he ain't got the city limits to stop him,' Wash said in a proud manner.

'Or some state border,' Chance added.

'That may be, son,' I said, before the two of them got me into all sorts of trouble, 'but don't you go volunteering me for duty trouble like you did when we chased after them horses of yours a few months back. By God, the Rio Grande is the Rio Grande, and I don't mind telling you that I got no interest in seeing how ornery them Federales can be. Not for some time to come.'

'Yeah,' Chance said with a sly grin, remembering his desperate try at getting back upwards of twenty horses he'd lost on the word of a trusting Confederate general named Shelby. But that's a whole 'nother canyon. 'That was a bit of excitement, wasn't it?'

'I'll say,' Wash agreed, and downed a good bit of the beer in his glass.

Drinks in hand, the lot of them began asking me what all a federal marshal could do, so I had to explain as best I could how far-reaching the authority of such a position was. I was only half winded when Asa Wilson, one of the local ranchers I knew, pushed aside a couple of men and took a stance before me.

Asa was nearly as old as I was. In fact I could remember his boys growing up with mine, although I couldn't say they were best of friends. Got downright mean with each other once or twice, but that was how boys were. It never did affect the friendly relationship Asa Wilson and I had with one another, though. Of that I was always glad, for I considered him a good man to ride the river with.

But the man standing before me now didn't look anything like the Asa Wilson I knew. Asa was normally a well-kept, clean-shaven man, and now he was dirty and dusty and looked tired as could be, an indication that he had been on the trail and doing a lot of outdoor riding. His face was a mite bloodied, a large cut on his left cheek that I gauged was put there by a hard right hand or the barrel of a pistol.

'Lordy, what happened to you, Asa?' I asked, taking in the battered man before me.

'Yeah, what the hell happened?' one of the men asked in astonishment.

'You been in a fight, Asa?' another man said.

'Listen,' Ernie Johnson said in a hard voice, 'you barflies just leave the man alone.' To me he said, 'Marshal, you get him to a table and I'll get him a drink. A good stiff one.'

I nodded in silence and helped Asa Wilson to an empty table off to the side. I made sure there wasn't going to be any eavesdropping if

I could help it. Chance and Wash picked up our half-empty beers and set them down at the table. I didn't say anything about wanting to keep this conversation with Asa private. Hell, they were my boys and I could trust them.

I undid Asa's kerchief and dabbed at the wound on his cheek while he sat there in silence, his only sound a painful wince when I touched a tender spot. Those seemed to be everywhere. Ernie was soon at the table, setting down new beers for me and my boys, and a water glass half filled with whiskey and a beer for Asa. The rancher gave the whiskey glass a greedy look, grabbed hold of it and chugalugged half the contents at once. I knew from past experience that if he had drunk half the glass of beer, why he'd have had steam shooting out of his nose, ears, and eyes all at once. Instead, he gently set the glass back down, closed his eyes for a few seconds and breathed a heavy sigh of relief. It almost seemed as though—for those few seconds, anyway—he was dead to the world, for when he got his vision straight again he looked at me as though seeing me for the first time. He sounded a whole lot more relaxed this time.

'I reckon I should congratulate you on your promotion,' he said, trying to sound as friendly as possible. It was a poor attempt, for he winced too often to sound convincing.

No, this wasn't the Asa Wilson I'd known so long.

'Now, Asa, you stop trying to flatter me,' I said. 'You know I don't take tampering with the law none too lightly.' I pulled his head back to take a look at him again. This time I spoke what was on my mind. 'Damn, you look like you come out second best in a bear fight, with only two contestants.'

'It don't matter, Will,' he said, his tired voice now matching the look of the man. 'It was almost worth it. Almost.'

'Asa, nothing ain't worth that bad a beating,' Chance said, speaking up for the first time since Asa had walked in on us.

'You ain't been where I have, Chance.' The rancher's voice took on a new tone, one of mean determination.

'Mr Wilson,' Wash said, 'I think you ought to just take it easy. You sure don't look in none too good a shape.'

'No, I've got to talk. If I don't, I may never get it all out.' I had a notion the more he talked the more tired he was getting.

'Well, you stop beating around the bush and spit it out then, Asa,' I said. 'Let's hear it afore you pass out in your beer.'

Asa Wilson took a sip of the beer and set it down.

'It's my boys, Jeremiah and Thomas,' he began. 'They're in a town up north. In jail.'

'Jail!'

8

'Damn sure betcha,' he replied with a nod. A pained look came to his face now, and it had me wondering if it was from the pain in his body or from the thought running through his mind. When I heard his next words, I knew for sure. '*Murder* they're saying! Can you beat that? *Murder!*'

'No,' Wash said in disbelief. 'Why, they had trouble killing food for the table, as I recall.' Wash was right. Asa Wilson's boys were as big and solidly built as my own, but their tempers had been a lot harder to rile than Chance's or Wash's. Part of it was their mother having been a Quaker in her upbringing, I reckon. Like my own wife, she was now dead. Frontier life was hard on women. I knew for a fact that it got to be a good deal harder on the men who had to raise their children all by themselves too.

Asa Wilson blinked hard now, finding it difficult to keep his eyes open. Either the whiskey or the pain was getting to him, and he didn't have long before he'd be passing out from one or the other.

'Wash,' I said, 'go tell Margaret to get a room ready, preferably one on the ground floor. Have her get her medicinals out while she's at it.' I glanced back at Asa. 'Won't be long now before he'll be so much dead weight.'

'You bet, Pa.' Wash swallowed a mouthful of beer and was gone.

9

'Asa, what say we get you to a place you can rest easy,' I said.

'No.' He shook his head adamantly. 'I gotta talk.'

'Good. We can do it on the way.'

He took a deep swallow of his water glass of whiskey, while Chance, never being one for waste, drank the rest of his beer as well as his brother's. By the time Asa was on his feet, Chance was on one side, I on the other, as we guided him out of the saloon.

'Just how far can one of you U.S. Marshals go, Will?' the rancher asked as he wobbled down the boardwalk toward the Ferris House.

'Ary I'm not mistaken, pretty far, Asa,' was my reply. 'Why do you ask?'

'I don't recall ever asking you much, Will,' Asa said, now oblivious of the pain, 'but I gotta tell you, my boys mean the world to me. You know that.'

'Sure, Asa. I know.'

'And they ain't killers, either,' he added.

'I know, Asa. I know.'

'I need you to help me get 'em out of that place. That town.'

Chance and I had been careful to guide him on the boardwalk and then across the street toward the Ferris House, the one and only boarding house in Twin Rifles. We almost had him to the door now.

'What town, Asa? Where is this town?' I

10

asked as we opened the door and got him across the threshold.

'My God, what happened to him?' Rachel asked once we were inside.

'Back here, boys.' The second voice was from her mother, Margaret. She'd seen a good share of men who looked less than pretty, so this sight didn't bother her as much as it did her daughter.

'Hogtown,' Asa said, then went limp in our arms. Chance easily picked up the man, as though he were a sack of potatoes, and disappeared from sight, down the hallway and off to the side.

'Did he say Hogtown?' Wash asked with a confused look about him.

'It sure did sound like it,' Chance said, returning from the back.

'Never heard of it.'

Chance shrugged and said, 'Neither have I.'

At which point they both looked at me for the answer, just like they had always done.

'You sure you want to know?' I said.

Both nodded with the same enthusiasm they showed for hard rock candy when it was being offered some twenty years before.

'Well, boys, if what I hear is right, it's hell with the hide off,' I said and raised an eyebrow.

Chance and Wash glanced at each other and then at me. I looked down at my chest, then thumbed the shiny new marshal's badge. When I glanced back at the two of them, none of us spoke.

We didn't have to.

We were all thinking the same thing.

CHAPTER TWO

I knew Asa Wilson would want me to get his boys back as soon as possible, but by the time Margaret and Rachel got through fussing over him, it was noon time and the day was half gone. The boys agreed with me that it was better to spend the rest of the day getting supplies together for the trip and get a fresh start on the trail tomorrow morning.

'We've got a long ways to go, and it's gonna take some gathering to put this little trip together,' I said as we took our places at the community table in the Ferris House. After my wife got killed by the Comancheros just before my boys had returned from the war this past spring, I didn't have the heart to go back to the little ranch we'd had outside of town.

Instead, I'd taken up residence in the Ferris House and turned the ranch—or what was left of it—over to my two boys, who were making a go of it now. Since lawman had never been the highest paying job around, I'd struck a deal with Margaret Ferris to supply wood in exchange for room, board and meals at her place.

At least once every few days, Chance would come to town to join me for a meal. It wasn't that he was looking for what they called some fancy kind of cuisine as much as it was the company of Rachel, whom he'd taken a liking to since returning from the war. Both Margaret's girl and my boy were the shy kind when it came to courting, which was fine by both of us. A body shouldn't rush into such things as marriage. A good foofaraw, well, Chance would be the first one to throw a punch at an event like that. But marriage, well, that was an iffy proposition at best to his way of thinking.

'I'll say,' Wash agreed. 'I'll have to check Kelly's Hardware this afternoon and see how much ammunition they can spare for us.'

'Don't get too much, Wash,' Chance said. 'Remember, we only got so much money on account with Kelly.' My boys had brought back a whole passel of rifles and pistols from a gang of Comancheros who thought they were tougher than we were made. It was near six months ago, and I'll never forget how we went into their camp and did them in. Hell, if they'd killed your wife, you'd do the same thing. Guaranteed! Never being one to let things go to waste, a primary lesson you learn real quick out here, we'd gathered up

13

the firearms, powder and ball and brought them back. My boys had traded them to Kelly's Hardware, half for cash and half for credit on future purchases. The economy being the way it was now that the war was over, I couldn't say as I blamed Chance for being on the cautious side.

'Where are you three off to now?' Rachel said as she set down three steaming plates of roast beef before us. Roast beef was one of Margaret's specialties, probably the best in the state. Neither one of the women bothered to ask the Carston clan what they'd like to eat anymore. They knew our tastes in beef and knew that we wouldn't haggle over anything they cooked, for both of them were excellent at the stove.

Rachel's question took me by surprise. 'How'd you know we were going someplace?'

It was Margaret who took to answering me. 'It may not seem obvious to you boys,' she said as she poured more coffee and set down a heaping plate of biscuits, 'but Rachel and I have decided that the only time all three of you ever show up at this table together, it's for some kind of war council. Isn't that what you call it?'

'Yeah, I reckon it is,' I said in reply, seeing her point.

'Besides,' Rachel added with a mischievous smile I believe women call coyness, 'if Wash was given his druthers, why, he'd be eating over across the street, so Sarah Ann could wait on him.'

Sarah Ann was the daughter of Big John Porter, who owned and operated the Porter Café. She was also the one and only waitress Big John had, and a right pretty young lady too, although she was only eighteen years old or so. Joshing my youngest boy about Sarah Ann was one sure way to bring a blush to his face. Of course, what Rachel was saying was true, for Wash seldom ate at the Ferris House anymore, now that he knew Sarah Ann.

'Oh,' I said, feeling the boy needed some kind of defending. 'You mean the same way Chance shows up here instead of at the Porter Cafe? Pure coincidence, I suppose.' My words brought a flush to Rachel's face, but I wasn't the only one doing some defending of offspring that day.

'Don't worry, honey,' Margaret said with a smile, 'Chance isn't courting you.' Her words surprised Chance as much as they did me. 'He's just been away to war too long, and is still getting his fill of what real homemade cooking tastes like.' She winked at Chance and me, adding, 'Eat your meals, boys, before they get cold.' Then she disappeared back into the kitchen area.

We did a good bit of eating before we did any more talking. Hot food was going to be a rarity where we were heading, so we ate what we could get now, knowing it would be some time before we'd have Margaret and Rachel—and Sarah Ann—to cook for us again. My boys had been in that damned war long enough, and I'd fought enough Indians and outlaws and thieves of one sort of another over my years to know better than to even bring up the question of the possibility of maybe not making it back. You start thinking like that out here, and you just might *not* make it back. So I discounted it as a damn fool notion to begin with, knowing my boys did the same.

All three of us had pushed our plates away and were discussing how many weapons to take along, and whether or not we thought Old Man Farley would let us use his pack mule for this expedition, when Margaret reappeared with her ever-present coffeepot.

'You never did say where you were heading,' she said as she filled our cups.

'There's some that might think you was being mighty nosy with questions like that, Miss Margaret,' Chance said. It sort of surprised me, Chance saying something like that. Or maybe he figured he'd had enough of a meal that noon.

Margaret's face took on a frown I'd only seen a handful of times before. It was the kind of look that said she meant business. 'Well now, Mr Carston,' she said in a formal

16

and stiff manner. 'Perhaps I should tell Rachel to cut your ration of roast beef sandwiches in half.'

From the expression on his face, you'd think Chance had just been kicked in his elsewheres, he looked that hurt.

'Wouldn't do any good, Miss Margaret,' his brother said. 'He'd just steal the ones you'd made for me.'

Funning around is one thing, but we had things to do this afternoon, and spending the rest of the day trading barbs with one another wasn't about to get them done any faster.

'I gauge we'll be heading up by the Canadian River, Margaret,' I said. 'Farther than we had to go when we hunted down those Comancheros this past spring. I figure we'll be the better part of a week getting there. Mostly, it'll depend on Mother and Father.'

'Mother and Father?'

'Mother Nature and Father Time,' I said. 'If Mother takes care of Nature and we don't get flooded out or worse, Father ought to give us the Time to get there in three, maybe four days of steady riding.'

'Does it have to do with Asa Wilson?' she asked, taking a real interest in our trek.

I said it did and filled her in on what information Asa had given me before passing out. According to Margaret, Asa was in need of a good deal of rest and feeding, for he had wolfed down a good portion of her roast beef before laying back down and falling asleep.

'He's bruised pretty bad, from what I've seen under his shirt,' she added, 'not to mention the ones on his face. He said he hadn't eaten in a couple of days either. I had Rachel feed him just as soon as she gave you fellas your plates.' She paused a moment in thought. 'He said something about Hogtown. Does that have anything to do with you?'

'That's where his boys are being held,' I said. 'Likely where we'll wind up.'

'Worse than that Hell City we went through,' Chance said, a determined look about him. A hand went to Margaret's mouth as she remembered the bloody details of our search for my wife's killers. Along the way we'd stopped at a place called Hell City, where I called in a marker on a man I used to know. We were lucky to get out of that place alive. But that's a whole 'nother canyon.

I dug an elbow hard and fast into Chance's side, giving him a hard look at the same time. 'You take some kind of perverted pleasure out of scaring women, do you?' I said in a less than considerate tone. He didn't like it, but he wasn't about to challenge me about it either. He knew better.

'We'll be all right, Margaret,' I said with a wink to her. 'You tell Rachel we'll be just fine.' I stood up and ran a coarse hand along the side of her smooth face. 'You just make sure you two are still here when we get back.'

I thought I saw a tear come to her eye as we left.

It took the better part of the afternoon to round up the necessities we were going to need for the trip to Hogtown, but we found out that Asa Wilson had a lot more friends than we thought he had. When Kelly found out what we were needing the ammunition for, he told Wash to stock up on as much as we needed and he'd take the loss, although I doubted that it would be that much. Hell, Kelly had the only hardware store in town.

It was the same story with Old Man Farley when I asked him for the use of his pack mule. Otis, the pack mule, was one of the strongest beasts I'd ever run across. I was sure I'd need him to pack as many supplies as possible on this trek up north. To my surprise, Old Man Farley agreed and gave me the loan of the animal with his blessing, especially once he found out why I was needing the pack mule.

While Wash and I were out doing our own chores that afternoon, I gave Chance the job of cleaning all of those extra rifles and pistols we were planning on taking. I've always thought Wash had more tact than his brother when it came to parleying with someone. If I knew Chance—and I thought I did, since I was the one who raised him, for the most part—he would have charged into Kelly's Hardware with a Colt in one hand and a rifle in the other and stuck both in Kelly's chest. Then he would have offered Kelly the deal of a lifetime by volunteering to give us the ammunition we'd need, or dying regretting it. I figured it was much safer having Chance stick with something he knew and liked—guns.

We were up bright and early that next morning. In fact, we were the first ones to find our way to Margaret's community table. But all three of us stopped in our tracks at the sight of Asa Wilson, battered and bandaged, just like Margaret had said, sitting at the community table all by himself, sipping a cup of steaming coffee.

'Have a seat boys,' he said in the same tone of voice I'd always known him to speak in. 'The ladies are expecting you.'

'Asa, what in the devil are you doing here?' I said, as flustered as my boys at the sight of the man.

'Yeah, you should be resting,' Chance added.

'Oh, come on, Will,' the man said in a tone of disbelief. 'You didn't think I'd let you go without me, did you?'

CHAPTER THREE

Any man who's willing to make a go of it on this frontier is going to have to be hale and hearty to begin with. He's going to have to be willing to take the punishment that Mother Nature can dish out at a moment's notice, and that isn't speaking kindly of Mother Nature; twisters and flash floods happen more often than a body would ever want to wish for in this land. Then there's the Indians, Comanch' to be specific. Somehow or other these back East idealists got the idea that this land was ours for the taking and, with God on our side, why, we shouldn't have any trouble at all doing just that. Well, hoss, don't you believe a word of it! Most land that was explored and settled in this world was usually inhabited and taken from someone else. The Comanche just happened to live in what us whites called Texas after we took it from the Mexicans. So much for history. The fact of the matter is that surviving the Comanch' is just as hard as surviving the fickleness of Mother Nature, sometimes harder.

Asa Wilson had survived all that and now had to deal with killers of a different sort. Seeing him sitting there at Margaret's community table as cool as a cucumber said a lot for the man's determination to get his two sons back alive. But then, I'd be doing the same thing if it was Chance and Wash in the fix his boys were in. Hell, the only way you really survive Mother Nature and the Comanch' and all the rest out here is by sticking with your family. That's what counts in a land like this. Loners don't last too long, no matter how those penny dreadfuls portray them. Asa Wilson had my respect as a man to ride the river with, sitting there as though nothing had happened and this was just one more day of living out here. Bandaged up or not, you can't fault a man for that kind of gumption.

'You sure you want to do this, Asa?' I said, taking a seat next to him. 'I'm the one who's the lawman, you know. It's my job.'

'I know that, Will, and I say this with no disrespect intended, but those are my boys up there. I *have* to go after 'em,' he said, a determined look about him.

'None taken, Asa. I understand. I understand exactly.' I meant it and Asa Wilson knew it. To my boys I said, 'Looks like we got one more rider.'

Chance smiled a bit and looked Asa right in the eye as he said, 'We got one more fighter, Pa, and that's gonna help out considerable if this Hogtown is as hell-bent as you say.'

Margaret is usually what you'd call

chipper in the morning. A good night's rest will do that for a body, I reckon. Margaret is usually that type of person. But this morning she was a bit more somber. Maybe women are like that. The farther away you're going and the longer you're going to be away, the quicker they get to missing you. I never have been able to figure that species out. I reckon that just ain't my best suit. If you know what I mean.

'Don't worry, Rachel, we'll be back soon,' Chance said. I reckon he'd seen the same thing in Rachel as she set a portion of ham and eggs before him. She looked like she might have been crying some, but I wasn't about to get into some argument over the way she looked. Ain't never seen the like of a woman and her looks. It was damn near as bad as dealing with some of these young squirts who came back from the war with a feeling for killing more than living. I'm glad I ain't got a big head like that. I could see that Chance was having the same problem with Rachel. He had a fork in one hand, ready to attack his food before the warmth of it went south on him, while Rachel had a desperate hold of his other hand. It looked like a toss-up between the affections of a woman and what Chance's belly was wanting. Me, I was betting on the food to go first.

'Looks like you'll have to be making a bit more food for us, Margaret, now that Asa's going along,' I said between mouthfuls of food. I happened to look up from my plate and there she was, just standing there, watching me eat. You'd think she'd never seen a man eat before. I found myself wondering why in the world she was standing there staring at me like that, but you can bet I wasn't about to pose the question. Hell, by the time she got through explaining her answer, why, I'd have cold food on my plate and it would be a couple hours past sunup.

'Now, Will Carston, you ought to know better than that,' was her reply, accompanied by the first smile I'd seen that day. Seeing it made me smile and added a bit of renewed hope to my purpose in life. 'Mr Wilson made his intentions known last night. I must admit,' she added, giving Asa a less than confident look as she spoke, 'that at first I tended to doubt his sanity, for a man in his shape shouldn't be going anywhere.' Her gaze now took in Chance, Wash, and me. 'But then I remembered that you Carston men have done similar things where relatives are concerned, and none of you is exactly the sanest person I've ever met'—here she cocked an eye at me—'so it seemed only fitting that Mr Wilson join your little group.' With that she made her way out of the room.

'Now, ain't that like a woman to go about saying things in a roundabout way,' I said, finishing off the rest of my meal.

'I'd keep an eye out for that woman, Will, if I was you,' Asa said with a smile.

'How's that?'

'Hell, any time a woman starts talking about how she doubts your sanity, the way Miss Margaret just did, why, it's a sure sign she's taking a liking to you,' he said, still holding the smile. 'Next thing you know, she'll be telling you to tuck in your shirttail. You can bet she means business then.'

I grumbled something in my coffee, but it was Chance who decided to pick up on Asa's comments.

'What's that, Pa, you say she's already tried that?' he chuckled.

I could feel the red start to crawl up my neck as he spoke. I reckon I just wasn't ready for that much funning this morning. 'Son,' I said with a frown, 'I do believe it's about time you checked old Otis out back. Working your mouth in here ain't gonna get you nothing but trouble. Why don't you try some honest work for a change?' Wash saw the wisdom in accompanying his older brother out back, leaving me and Asa alone at the table.

'You still carrying that Henry rifle, Asa?' I said, trying to change the subject. He nodded, still chewing a biscuit, and I added, 'Good, you can share my ammunition.' I carried a Henry rifle too.

25

'She really is a nice lady, Will.'

'I know, Asa, I know,' I said. Then I reached down inside me and told him something I hadn't shared with anyone else, not even my boys. 'And I'd be a liar if I didn't admit to liking her some too, Asa. Maybe sometime in the future we'll talk about more than just the way she cooks her food. But try to remember that it's only been six months since I put the women I've spent near half of my life with in the ground.' I paused, took a sip of coffee and looked back at him in a sincere way. 'She ain't an easy woman to forget, Asa. You should know that.'

What had started out as fun wasn't funny any more, at least not for Asa once he'd heard me out. A somber look came to his face and he spoke with an apologetic voice. 'I'm sorry, Will, I forgot it was still that touchy for you.' He paused a moment, and I knew by his expression that he was going back in his own reverie. 'Believe me, I remember how it was. Been ten years now since Ginny passed away.' He smiled at me in a sheepish way. 'I still think about her once in a while. Still miss her. I reckon women like ours you don't ever really forget.'

I nodded silently. His words were truer than he might have thought. Hell, if I hadn't remembered the things I'd learned from my wife as she was bringing up our boys, I likely

26

wouldn't have been any good at dealing with Chance and Wash when they'd come home from the war. As it was, I still found myself thinking about Cora, even when I was around Margaret.

When we stepped outside, I knew it wouldn't be long before the sun would be up. It was time to get on our way, but I had a couple of things to do first. One was to stop by the office and check with Joshua, my deputy, who would be in charge of the town while I was gone. He had a bit of a growth of beard that never got trimmed all the way, and truth to tell, he looked more like one of those hill folk than any plainsman I'd ever run across, but he knew how to handle himself, and I felt comfortable leaving the town in his hands. What I instructed him to do was see the bank manager about taking some money out of my account later that morning and resupplying Margaret Ferris for the coffee and food she was preparing for me, my boys, and Asa Wilson. There are some things that chopping a cord of wood just won't replace, and the supplies to run a boardinghouse is one of them.

I returned to the horses and Chance, Wash, and Asa with an armful of rifles, and a bunch of pistols stuck in my waistband. It only took a couple of minutes to sort them all out so everyone had their own weapons. Chance probably had more six-guns than the lot of us. But then, I couldn't blame him. Between that expedition we'd been on hunting down the killers of my Cora, and that trek we made into Mexico not long ago, why, Chance spent more ammunition than anyone I've ever seen. He just purely liked a good gunfight. Or maybe it was the war that made him a more tenacious fighter. Whatever the reasoning behind it, I knew I could count on him to hold his end in any kind of a fight. Although I don't recall telling him since he'd returned from the war, I was damn proud of him. Hell, I was damn proud of both of my boys!

When Chance had first come back from the war, he was working on making his own holster, which came in right handy when you considered how clumsy that old cavalry holster he had was. The boy turned out to be right good at it. Fact is, both Wash and me asked him to try his handiwork fashioning similar holsters for us. When he hadn't been working that ranch he and his brother were putting together, Chance had done a fine job of making holsters for the both of us. The Remington .44 I carried felt right good in that newfangled holster, although I was still getting used to drawing from my right side instead of the cross draw I had been used to as a ranger.

'Here,' Chance said, holding out a piece of leather that looked as though he had fashioned it. I was getting ready to put an extra Remington .44 into my saddlebags when he caught my attention.

'What do you want me to do with that?' I asked in a confused way.

'Put the Remington in this and tuck it away in your saddlebags, Pa,' he said. 'Hand over your holster and gun belt tonight when we make camp, and I'll show you how I'm gonna set this holster on your left hip. By the time we get a day or two up north, I wouldn't be surprised if you'd be needing it.'

I didn't doubt the truth in what he said, for this wasn't a Sunday social we were going to, that was for sure. What did surprise me was him giving his brother the same thing as he gave me.

'What about me?' Asa asked as we mounted up. 'Looks like you boys have got two or three times more guns than I do.' I wasn't sure whether the sound in his voice was filled with envy or helplessness.

'Well, if nothing else, you can always load while we fire,' Chance said with that smart-alecky grin of his. He seemed to be having a whole lot of fun at other people's expense this morning. I made a note to correct that sometime in the future.

Asa Wilson wasn't sure just how to take it. One thing was sure as we started out, though. Asa wasn't any keener on my oldest son's sense of humor than I was.

Yes, I was definitely going to have to correct that.

CHAPTER FOUR

We put in a good thirty miles that day. Not as much as one of those Pony riders they used to have carrying the mail before the war, but then it wasn't bad for having a pack mule along with us. I don't know if Old Man Farley whispered something in Otis's ear before we left or what, but the animal seemed to be pretty accommodating that day. If we hadn't had Otis in trek, we likely could have made fifty to a hundred miles, for the horses we had were mustang bred and had a lot of bottom. Trouble is that after you run a good horse that hard in one day, it's likely to need a bit of resting the next, so we took it easy on the horses, knowing they'd have to last us not only the ride to Hogtown, but the ride back as well.

We didn't do much at noon camp but take a swig or two of precious water and chew on a biscuit or two Margaret had provided, as we tried to jog our memories as to any water holes that might be in the area we were passing through. It was times like this that I took to wondering what it was that Houston, Austin, and all the rest saw in a land like this when they proclaimed freedom for all Texicans back in '36. Hell, the mountains ain't much more than hills if you compare 'em to them Shinin' Mountains I spent my earlier youth in. You'd have to fight over the decent grassland in the state—which some folks were beginning to do, if what I heard was correct—for the population was getting bigger every day and the portion of grassland was getting smaller and smaller to those wanting to farm that land. The land in the western portion of the state, the area we were going to be traveling in, was more desert than anything else, complete with cactus, sparse water holes, and devilish mean sun in the right seasons of the year. It was getting into late fall now; still and all, by noon camp I'd discarded that buckskin jacket of mine. The sun was high and hot, and the only shade I could find was under the brim of my John B., and that wasn't much.

No sir, the lay of this land in West Texas wasn't much to look at and less to appreciate, that much was true. But I knew in the back of my mind that I'd gone over this same question in better days, the kind of days when my boys and I had spent a good part of the day just fishing with nary a worry in the world, and I'd reasoned exactly why Houston and Austin and all the rest had done what they did. The words Liberty and Freedom have always meant something special to people who call themselves Americans. They stir the soul and bring forth in men a vision of how things could be, how they'd like them to be. They summon courage in such men as Bowie and Crockett and Travis, but more important, they summon a vision of the future for their children and the life they could have. Even with a land as barren as that our horses were traveling over now, they had a vision and a dream that they could make something out of it, no matter how impossible it seemed. I reckon that's the difference between idealism and reality for you; one's a nice goal to have in the back of your mind, as long as you know full well that it may be your children, maybe even your grandchildren, who finally realize the dream.

I'd long since pinned my brand new marshal's badge to the inside of my breast pocket on my shirt, a lesson I'd learned long ago in this land. A piece of tin as shiny as that new badge would ricochet the sun a goodly distance in a land as flat as that we were on. Me, I didn't have a hankering to draw any more crowds than I had to. No sir.

'Say, I wouldn't want to bother you, Will,' Asa said when we decided to make camp at the end of the day, 'but you are gonna put that badge back on sometime, ain't you?'

'You know, Asa, I recall Mother telling me that there is a time and place for everything,'

I said with raised eyebrow, just to let him know that he was bothering me a mite. 'Of course, I was a young man at the time, and she was talking about courting and such. Daddy had told me the same thing when I was a mite younger. I recall that was one day when he took me hunting and I got a mite anxious with him about the game we were after.'

'What are you getting at, Will?'

'What I'm getting at, Asa, is this,' I said, my cocked eyebrow turning into a frown. 'I'm long since over my courting manners. That means I'm hunting, Asa. Humans, not animals, mind you, but hunting just the same. Like Daddy said, there's a time and place for everything, so don't you worry, I'll have my badge on when the time comes.' Before he could reply, I leaned a bit closer to him and, in a lower voice, added, 'And don't you say a damn thing about Margaret.'

'I understand,' was his reply, a wise one at that.

*　　　*　　　*

It had been a long day and we were all fairly tired, so we made a pot of coffee and ate some of Margaret's roast beef sandwiches. The only thing that went wrong with the meal was Chance and his sense of humor.

'Courting days, huh?' he said, when he'd

33

finished his meal. He'd wisely taken to squatting down across the fire from me, well out of arm's length. I had a mouthful of food at the time and didn't do much more than mumble through it at his comment, although I thought I saw a bit of caution in the eyes of Wash and Asa. 'You ought to start practicing them courting manners, Pa,' he added with a smirk I immediately disliked. 'I gauge you'll be needing them right soon with Miss Margaret.' If he was trying to get my goat, he was succeeding. But I wasn't about to throw decent coffee and good food at him, much as I wanted to. I simply sat there and gave him a long hard stare as the red crept up my neck, slow but steady. Wash and Asa had the good sense not to make a fuss about the whole thing or get involved in any way, shape, or form. Me, I was going to get involved in Chance and his sense of humor. Real involved.

After supper Wash and I shucked our gun belts and holsters and turned them over to Chance. As he'd said earlier in the day, he took out his bowie knife and did a careful job of slicing two straight lines on the left side of the gun belt, each one about two inches parallel to the other. The best way to describe it is to say that, as seen from the holster in its upright position, they ran from northeast to southwest. Chance then took each of the holsters he'd given us that morning and fit them through the slats so they would sit on the gun belt in the proper position to hold a holstered gun in a cross draw from the left side. It looked real good, and when I tried it on, felt just as comfortable, although a mite heavier once the Remington was added.

'Thanks, Chance,' I said once I had the holster in place, 'I appreciate it.' I adjusted it around some, as though having some trouble with it while he looked on from his squatting position. 'There's just one thing.'

'What's that?' he said, a smile of gratitude on his face. Chance always was proud of what he did.

'This,' I said, and let out a right cross that sent him flying ass over teakettle on his back. 'Smart ass,' I said as I shook my fist and Chance rubbed his jaw line, both of us looking for a bit of relief from the pain we'd incurred.

'What did you go and do that for?' he asked, looking totally astonished, as though he hadn't the foggiest idea of what brought on my actions.

'I *don't* appreciate your smart-alecky remarks about me and Miss Margaret, sonny,' I said in a hateful voice that matched the look on my face. 'I'd learn something about courting manners before I started making light of 'em, Chance. Besides, you make ary so much as a comment about that again, in private or mixed company, don't make no never mind, and I'll finish this fight. And that's that.'

And it was.

Chance wandered off to look after the horses, or so he said. When he was out of earshot, Wash got right curious.

'Why'd you wait that long to hit him, Pa?' he asked. 'I don't recall you ever putting up with that much guff from Chance before.'

'Your memory must be fading, son,' was my reply. When Wash gave me a confused look I added, 'Chance said he was gonna take care of this holster modification, as I recall.' I hefted the newly redesigned holster on my hips and smiled. 'Feels right good, if I do say so my own self. It's like this, Wash. My mama didn't raise no fool.'

My son smiled then, seeing what I'd been getting at, knowing that if I'd hit Chance earlier, why, the boy had a hot temper and likely wouldn't have done anything to that holster of mine. No sir.

'Ain't that the truth,' Asa said with a smile, and unrolled his blankets.

Chance was quiet as a church mouse the next morning. Sulky was a better way of putting it. But then, I reckon no one like being cut off at the knees, especially loudmouths and experts. Chance tended toward being a bit of both. As far back as I could remember, it was his mouthing off that had gotten him in some of the more serious fights in his lifetime; and I don't believe I ever saw anyone who was better at fixing or handling a firearm, so I reckon my oldest boy was a bit of an expert too.

I didn't think an awful lot of Chance for his raw sense of humor and the way he'd tried to push it on me the previous night, but as it turned out, I was right glad that he'd rigged my holster with room for that second Remington. Right glad.

A stretch of land in the area we were heading for was known as the Comanche Trail. It runs north by south for the most part and is inhabited by Comancheros, who ply their trade on it with the Comanche Indians of the area. Chance and Wash and I had come across these Comancheros about six months back, when we were hunting down the dogs who'd killed my Cora. Like I say, I wasn't hunting trouble, for I knew there would be enough for all of us where we were headed. But I also knew that if those Comancheros had dared to venture as far south as Twin Rifles, why, they might be anywhere in between my hometown and Hogtown. Me, I was going to keep an eye peeled for those varmints just in case we ran across them before we got to Hogtown, and said as much to Asa Wilson and my boys when we headed out that morning. Asa and Wash acknowledged me, but Chance only grunted.

Comancheros never are too hard to identify. They tend toward some of the fancies a Mexican will sport on his clothing; spangles and silver gewgaws that make them appear audacious to anyone within sight. Leather boots, usually stolen, or leggings. Shirts and vests with more gewgaws, all topped off with a Mexican sombrero or maybe a bandanna tied around their head and knotted in the back. Makes them look like they've just come off a raid with that old pirate Laffite, the fellow who used to make Galveston island his headquarters. But what really caught your eye was the amount of weaponry they carried! Why, they looked like a walking armory, each and every one of them. Two or three pistols stuck in their belt, bandoleros of ammunition and a rifle in one hand and a bowie knife in the other. Don't ask them how they managed the reins of their mount, for the horses were usually as well trained at following orders as the men riding them were of killing at the drop of a hat. And every bit of what they had, from horse to hat, was stolen. To say I didn't care for them was putting it mildly!

Like I said, wearing a bunch of that gaudy shiny stuff can make you stand out something fierce. We were about to cross a trail a local stage line was using, when I saw a lot of flash and glitter from the hillside on the far side of the trail.

'Goddamn,' I heard Asa say as we pulled our horses to a halt.

'Betcherass!' Chance all but yelled, that crazy gleam in his eye. That Union army must have really been glad to have someone as crazy as Chance to go into battle with, even though most Texans fought for the Confederacy. The boy was already pulling out his Colts and checking the loads in them, getting ready to trade lead.

At first I thought Chance was planning on taking on the whole dozen or so of them in sight, which I really hadn't wanted in the first place. Like I said, I was trying to avoid a fight at the moment. Then I heard the stagecoach and knew that I couldn't stay out of it, whether I wanted to or not. Hell, I was a lawman, and those fellows sitting on the hill sure weren't planning a friendly reception for that stagecoach. Not with as many rifles in sight as they had, no sir!

'How do you want to do this, Will?' Asa asked me as he pulled out his Henry rifle.

'Git them bandits afore they git the coach, I reckon,' was all I could think to say. 'Hell, if we go charging in on this side of the coach, that guard is likely to shoot us out of the saddle, figuring us for more bandits.'

'Now you've got the idea,' Chance said, and spurred his horse, taking a head start on the rest of us, heading straight for the band

39

of Comancheros who were now coming down the rise at the stagecoach and us.

'Well, what're you waiting for!' I yelled back over my shoulder, taking off after my oldest son. Right or wrong, he had a plan in mind. It was a mite dangerous one at that, but at least it was a plan, and that's a hell of a lot better than just sitting on your keister waiting for something to happen.

After I'd come back from the Mexican War, I'd become a Texas Ranger. When Chance and Wash were old enough, I'd initiated them into the rangers and given them a lesson in growing up on this frontier. They knew just as much about rangering now as I did, and that counted for something, even when Chance took off like he just had, riding hell for leather toward a bunch that outnumbered us two to one. He had sand, I had to give him that.

One of the stories I always told my boys was how John Coffee Hays, one of the best rangers who ever lived, took a handful of rangers—twenty some, I believe it was—and charged straight into a band of two hundred Mexican lancers who would have annihilated some of General Zachary Taylor's foot soldiers, and purely obfusticated them! They shot their way into the center of those mounted men and thoroughly confused them. Then they shot their way right back out, and only had one man as a casualty!

40

Saved the day, as they put it in those fairy tales. I was remembering that story now as I saw Chance doing the same thing old Jack Hays and his boys had done. Mind you, it wasn't two hundred men he was going up against, but he was outnumbered, that much was for sure.

I do believe we would have gotten shot out of the saddle if the four of us hadn't cut across that stagecoach path a good thirty yards before the coach came down the road. I found myself real glad Chance had fixed that new holster up on my left hip, for I was going to need that second Remington real bad.

I sat up straight and tucked the reins to my horse into my waistband and said a prayer that they'd stay there. Then I pulled out that second Remington and, two guns in hand, took aim on the yahoos heading our way. Chance was only three or four yards ahead of me and a mite to my right, so I saw the two men he shot fall from their mounts, knowing they were dead before they hit the ground. Like I said, Chance is an expert with those six-guns. I fired three shots and accomplished the same thing, both men dead by the time they left their mounts.

What made me nervous was the pilgrim who shot my hat off as he passed, along with the gunfire that was going on to my rear. I was expecting to feel a slug going through

41

my back any second now, knowing those damned Comancheros would kill a body any way they could. I stuck one gun back in its holster while I grabbed hold of the reins and wheeled my horse around to see what was going on. We'd ridden right through them, Chance and me, just like old Jack Hays had done!

I felt a mite easier when I saw that Wash and Asa had thinned the ranks of the Comancheros by one each as they'd ridden in on the flanks of Chance and me. Looked like one of those spears, the way we'd gone into that bunch of bandidos. Yes sir. But the real hero turned out to be that stagecoach driver, who was now standing up in his boot and pumping lead into the rather unorganized group of men who rode past him. They weren't looking to rob the stagecoach anymore, just wanting to get the hell out of the territory.

'Looks like their game went south on 'em, Pa,' Chance said, out of breath, his six-gun still in hand.

'I'd gauge they're heading south too,' Asa said with a smile of satisfaction.

Neither one of them looked worse for wear, although Chance looked as though he had a nick on his left leg. I was going to mention it to him, when it crossed my mind that Wash was nowhere in sight.

'Where's—' I started to say, but was

42

interrupted by a rifle shot that I knew at once to be that of Wash's Colt's Revolving Rifle. I tracked the sound to just past the now stopped stagecoach, somewhere in the vicinity of where we'd come from. Then I heard the braying of a mule, Otis to be exact, and recalled that we'd left the mule all by his lonesome when we'd lit out after the Comancheros. Remington still in hand, I lit out for Wash's location.

When I came on him, he had dismounted and was petting Otis, trying to calm him down.

'You all right, boy?' The worry in my voice was immediately eased when I didn't see any blood on Wash. The boy had been through a war and all, but he was still my youngest son. Like I said, there are some mothering habits I picked up from my Cora.

'Got the son of a bitch,' was all he said, pointing his rifle toward another dead body that I took to be a Comanchero.

'What happened?'

'Why, I just saved your life, Pa, that's when happened,' the boy said with a grin. Between him and Asa there seemed to be a lot of that stuff going around of late.

'Do tell,' I said, wondering what in the hell he was talking about.

'Why sure, Pa. After those Comancheros cut and run, I seen one of 'em trying to get hold of Otis here. Must've seen all those supplies, I reckon. I dusted him out of his saddle, and saved your life.'

'Son, what in the hell are you talking about?' I said, getting just a mite flustered at the whole situation.

'Well, think a minute, Pa. If you'd lost old Otis here—or worse, he'd gotten killed—why, Old Man Farley wouldn't care what kind of badge you wear. He'd be wanting to make a new addition to Potter's Field. So you see...'

Wash was right, for Otis was next to a human being for Old Man Farley, and everyone knew it. Hell, Otis was the only friend that the old man had in this world. And if he lost him...

'Yeah, I know, you saved my life.' Chance and Wash were both smiling now at what had happened. Asa Wilson was the only one I had left to say it to, so I did. 'Ain't nothing like when we was kids, Asa,' I said, shaking my head in defeat.

'Ain't that the truth,' he said. Then, breaking out in a wide grin, he added, 'Smart-alecky kids.'

CHAPTER FIVE

Otis wasn't any the worse for wear for the fracas he'd gotten into, which made me feel a

44

whole lot better about handing the mule back over to Old Man Farley once our journey was completed. Still, in the back of my mind was the lingering thought of how I was going to keep this animal alive until then. I'd be lying if I didn't admit to shooting a horse out from under a man at some time during my career as a lawman. It's a real shame to do that too. Hell, I usually felt worse about shooting the horse than I did the man riding it. I also knew that there were men where we were headed who wouldn't hesitate one bit to do the very same thing to me, and they likely didn't exclude pack mules from any animal shooting they'd do. Yes sir, I'd keep an eye out for Otis.

Chance was a different matter. I hadn't questioned either of my boys about what exactly they'd done in that damn war they were off fighting, figuring that when the time would come when they felt like talking about it, I'd be there to listen to them. I reckon that's one of the jobs you take on as a parent, being there when the kids get past the hand-holding stage and prefer to be treated like adults, and being a friend to them when they need one. I didn't know whether Chance had been shot during his time in the Union army, but he'd sure managed to get plugged a couple of times since he'd been back. I reckon that's the price you pay for charging into a bunch of buzzards with your guns blazing. Most times they're shooting right back at you!

Wash and Asa and me rounded up the horses these dead fellows wouldn't have any use for anymore and went through their saddlebags, finding just what I was looking for, a couple bottles of whiskey. Not that we were needing something to keep us warm around the camp fire, you understand. Coffee was always a good warmer-upper for me and my boys. Medicinal purposes is what I was needing the whiskey for. The truth of the matter is that on this frontier a body was hard put to find the kind of medicinals used by those big-city hospitals back East, so you made do the best you knew how. Whiskey was still one of the best germ and pain killers I'd found thus far. If you're thinking I ought to feel some guilt about stripping a dead man of a whiskey bottle, well, son, when it comes to saving the lives of my family, I tend to rid my mind of everything else other than getting them fixed up. And slight as Chance's wound was, he still needed fixing up.

'I don't know who you fellas are,' the stage driver said when we returned from our whiskey-hunting venture, 'but I'd like to thank you for helping out.'

'Carrying mail, were you?' I asked.

'Mail and passengers,' he acknowledged with a nod.

46

'That being the case, I was supposed to help you out,' I said, and produced my new U.S. Marshal's badge. 'Ary I recall right, robbing the mail's a federal offense.' Those Comancheros were likely interested in the passengers on this coach and any valuables they might have had, not to mention the women aboard. But I recalled seeing flyers circulating on some men who had tried robbing the Pony Express of its mail back in '60 and '61. The U.S. government didn't take kindly to people stealing their mail, for the warrants were still good on those bandits, even if the Pony was no longer in operation. The passengers, two men and a middle-aged woman, were unharmed, as was the driver.

The bullet had apparently just grazed the outside of Chance's thigh and wasn't as bad as it appeared at first. The trouble with some flesh wounds is they can be worse than a good clean wound. I wasn't about to tear away Chance's pants, much less have him take them off with a woman present, so I settled for cutting away a small patch of the material around the wound. Propped up against the wheel of the stagecoach, I had him take a good long pull on the contents of the bottle, then poured a good dollop of it on the wound as he let out a belch. The belch and the cussing I knew Chance would do sort of met in his throat, producing an odd sound I'd never heard before. However, it didn't keep the woman from turning beet red when she heard it. I had Wash unpack an extra bandanna I'd tucked away for just such an occasion, and tied it around Chance's upper leg, hoping to stifle the flow of blood, which was minimal to begin with. Healing would be the hardest part of this wound, but both Chance and I felt he could ride without much trouble. With that kind of determination, something told me my boy had indeed been wounded in one way or another during that war. I had the distinct feeling that more than once he'd been a man with a mission, and the mission came first, no matter what.

Asa and I decided to keep at least two of the horses, just in case Jeremiah and Thomas didn't have mounts when we got to Hogtown. The rest of the mounts I persuaded the stage driver, whose name I never did get, to take along with him to the next relay station. Stage companies were always complaining about the high price of horse flesh, and these were in good shape and free to boot! Besides, a body should never take to wasting good horse flesh.

We stripped the dead men of their powder and ball, rifles and knives, and left them where they lay, hoping that if any of their compadres returned to the site, they'd take the warning and not go tangling with any more stagecoaches. As for the weapons, I

48

wasn't about to give those birds an edge on us by letting them come back and strip their dead of their weapons so they could come after us. No sir.

All it takes is one run-in with the Comancheros to find out they're pretty much like a pack of wolves. They run in packs and rely on the old theory that there is strength in numbers. If ever you come across one of them all by his lonesome, you can damn sure bet that he has a whole passel of his compadres behind the nearest bush or rise. He'll wait until your back is turned to him and then back-shoot you or plant a knife in you. Mind you, now, I'll play fair as much as the next man, but when you come across scum like these fellows, well, if you care to survive, you'd best play by their rules. And they don't have any rules. That being the case, I sort of twisted around Mother's definition of the Golden Rule: *Do unto others before they do unto you.*

Having Otis along had added to the amount of time we would be able to cover ground, but I wasn't going to complain, for as far apart as some of these water holes were, we were going to need as much extra water as possible, and Otis was the one carrying it. I'd brought along eight extra canteens, two for each of us, mostly to keep the horses going across these dry stretches of desert. Adding those two horses to our cavvy

49

slowed us down a mite more that day, although we did make about ten more miles before finding a water hole suitable to our needs.

Patching up Chance didn't change his disposition toward me once the fight was over. He was still grumbling to himself and doing his best to ignore me. It was amazing how much his attitude could change from the first indication of a good brawl to after it was all over. I was beginning to think he'd taken to grudge fighting, which I never did care for. Believe me, between figuring out how I was going to handle Chance and what kind of move, if any, those Comancheros would make toward us, I had my hands full the rest of the day.

It was pushing sundown when we ate the evening meal, which consisted of more of Margaret's roast beef sandwiches and a pot of coffee. It had been another long day, and none of us was all that fired up about hunting up a scrawny prairie chicken or jack-rabbit. It would have been easy to pass it all off as part of the fight we were in that morning, but truth to tell, it was just plain hot that afternoon, and heat will take the starch out of any man.

Chance ate in silence again, still giving me hard glances every once in a while that said he was not over the run-in we'd had the previous night. 'I'm gonna check the horses and Otis,' he said when he was finished eating.

It was dark by then, and Wash made a move to go after his brother, but I put a steady hand on his arm and slowly shook my head. 'Let him be, son,' I said. 'He's likely just brooding. Besides, he's gonna have to work this out for himself.' Wash knew what I was talking about and didn't go any farther.

Like I said, you've got to keep an eye out for those Comancheros. Wash sat there and listened to Asa and me as we reminisced about bringing up our boys. All three of us must have gotten so enthralled with what we were talking about that we'd forgotten what was going on around us. It was Asa, sitting across the fire from me, who first noticed the man as he stepped out of nowhere behind me. I could see the fear in his eyes and knew it was trouble, whatever it was. In the flick of an eye I was on my feet, a hand planted on the palm of my Remington. The only reason I stopped in my tracks was because I heard him cock his own six-gun.

'You will kindly pull your gun out by the butt and set it down on the ground,' he said with a leer that went with his guttural-sounding voice. 'The Remington is a good gun.' I recognized him as one of the yahoos who attempted to stop the stagecoach this morning. Hell, when you're born with a face as ugly as this hombre's, and then add a jagged scar across a cheek, well, it's hard to forget no matter how hard you try.

I don't mind telling you I hate these sons of bitches with a passion. They'd killed my Cora, and I was filled with hate for the shiftless breed of killers that they were. Chance and Wash weren't exactly filled with love for these heathens either.

'I can't do that,' I said in a steady voice. No sooner had I spoken the words than a half dozen more of the varmints appeared on the far side of camp. I reckon the sight of them was supposed to ensure a quick death if I didn't comply with their wishes. Taking in the sight of them, it crossed my mind that Ugly must have rounded up a few friends to help him avenge the death of his compadres. 'Sorry, friend, I just can't do it,' I added. 'Your kind killed the woman I spent the better part of my life loving.'

'That's a fact, amigo,' Wash said. 'You're tangling with the wrong man tonight. Of course, she was my mother too, so you *really* stepped in it.' Wash was talking over his shoulder, facing the handful who had appeared in the shadows of the fire on the other side of camp. Asa had a determined look with a mite of worry thrown in for good measure. Me, I was just getting mad.

'Amigo, my ass.' The words came out in a deep growl that had a good deal of hatred in it. They came from right behind Ugly and they came from Chance, who was just a tad out of the light of the camp. Ugly, the Comanchero with the gun in hand, got a worried look on his face real quick like as he turned to face Chance behind him. He died with that worried look about him, as Chance put a bullet in his heart.

As soon as the Comanchero had begun to turn toward Chance, Wash and I had gone for our guns. By the time I had cleared leather and gotten off my first shot, I felt something tug at the buckskin jacket I'd put back on now that it was cooling off. What I didn't feel was pain, so I stood my ground and kept on firing my Remington. By the time I'd fired my second shot, wounding one of the bandidos, three of them were falling to the ground. Chance had his Colt's Army Model in action behind me, and Wash had yanked out that Dance Brothers six-gun he took so much stock in, and was blazing away at these yahoos too. We must have rattled these fellows something fierce, for the most they seemed to be doing was shooting wild and kicking up dust around us.

One of their shots did find a mark, though. Asa was drawing his gun and diving for some cover behind a dead log when the ball had opened. He'd yanked out his own pistol and hit the ground when a slug hit him high in the back of his shoulder. He only fired one round from where he lay, but he damn sure made it count from what I could see.

He was laying about five feet in front of me when he lifted his pistol up and cocked it, a look of pain grimacing his face. But he wasn't aiming it at the men who'd come to kill us. No sir. He was aiming it in the direction of Chance, a movement that purely threw me. I was about to turn my gun on Asa when he fired. I heard a grunt behind me as one more Comanchero, one who apparently had been sneaking up on Chance from the side of the camp and nearly made it, fell to the ground.

Wash had drawn his second gun, a Le Mat, and proceeded to walk toward the Comancheros laying dead or dying across the camp, firing into any body that moved. The boy was right. These fellows had stepped in it bad, for Wash was filled with as much contempt for them as Chance and me.

Asa had the only real wound our group got that night. I not only had a hole in my John B., but in my buckskin jacket as well. Neither Chance nor Wash had been hit. But Asa seemed in real pain as I rolled him over and surveyed his wound.

'Get that bottle of whiskey out of my saddlebags,' I said to no one in particular as I drew my bowie knife and laid it on the fire a minute. By the time I'd gotten Asa's shirt off, Chance had returned with the whiskey.

'I owe you one, Asa,' he said, setting the bottle down next to me. In a way his words surprised me, for Chance wasn't the humblest of men. To me he said, 'I could sure use a shot of that whiskey.'

'You wait till I get through with it first, boy,' was my reply, a rather curt one at that.

I offered Asa a good healthy swallow of the whiskey, but he refused. Most of his drinking had been in the line of beer. Chance and Wash knew what had to be done. Asa was laying on his belly now, and Chance took hold of his arms, keeping them still as I tried to take that bullet out. Wash had the bottle in hand and poured a generous dollop of the whiskey over the blade of my bowie when I took it off the fire. Then I started digging.

I don't know how much longer it took, but I finally got the slug out of Asa's back. He'd lost some blood and was a mite weak, but he was a tough old bird, and I knew that he'd get over this wound, if nothing else than for the pleasure of getting his boys out of jail in Hogtown.

When Wash covered him with a blanket, I poured my coffee cup about half full of whiskey and passed the bottle to Chance and Wash, adding some of the remains of our coffee to the cup.

'Boys, I need to tell you something,' I said, giving brief thought to what was on my mind. It had come to me while I was searching for that bullet in Asa, and it occurred to me that Asa shouldn't be the only one to know it.

'What's on your mind, Pa?' Wash asked.

'It's about women ... and your mother,' I said with a certain amount of caution. Wash glanced at his brother and shrugged. 'I know that I josh you boys about Rachel and Sarah Ann. Hell, you're young and you've got a few things to learn about love. I know I was that way.

'I started learning about love when I married your mother way back when. Ary you're lucky, you'll find a woman who loves you as much as Cora loved me.'

'What are you getting at, Pa?' Chance said, although I didn't notice any sarcasm in his voice now. It was softer than usual, as though he were trying to understand me. I hoped I was right.

'What I'm getting at, son, is that ... well, Margaret Ferris is one hell of a good-looking woman. I ain't denying that. But whether anything ever comes of her and me, I don't know. Not now, anyway. You see, your mother's only been dead six months. I still think about her a lot, still ain't used to being without her.'

'You miss her a lot, don't you, Pa?' Wash said.

I nodded silently.

'I think we all do, Pa,' Chance said in as

soft a voice as I'd ever heard him speak. He was silent a moment, in thought, before adding, 'I reckon I see why you took a poke at me the other night. I won't josh you about it anymore.'

'Thanks, son, I appreciate it.'

I finished my coffee, and the boys took the last few swigs of the whiskey bottle.

I think we all slept a lot better that night.

CHAPTER SIX

I was up a mite earlier than usual and took my time making breakfast, throwing a few pieces of bacon on the fire and setting aside some of Margaret's homemade biscuits to sop the grease with. I know that doesn't sound like much compared to some of those full-course meals you could find at the Ferris House or the Porter Café for a morning repast, but you'd be surprised how far a couple of strips of bacon, a biscuit or two and some good strong coffee will take a fellow.

Then there was the matter of Asa and Chance, both of whom were wounded to one extent or another, both of whom would be needing a bit more time than usual to get up and get going this morning. Asa was still a mite weak, but didn't hesitate to put away a few strips of bacon and some of Margaret's biscuits. Two cups of coffee apiece was about all we were likely to get out of that coffeepot of mine, although Asa was real thirsty, even after his own two cups. I set his canteen down next to him and told him to drink water afterward. I also made a mental note to refill his canteen before we broke camp that morning.

'I'll get your horse for you, Chance,' Wash said, while Chance was still eating. The words purely obfusticated the older brother, who was soon choking on his food, something you don't see happen too often with Chance. Hell, the food never stays in his mouth that long!

'Better be easy on those words, Wash,' I said, slapping Chance on the back a time or two. 'I do believe your brother found them as hard to swallow as he did his food.' Wash was the only one who walked away smiling. Like I said, Asa was busy drinking water, and Chance was still choking. Me, I was fighting like the devil himself trying to keep a straight face.

The sun was up by the time we got saddled to ride. But at least Asa and Chance weren't complaining about getting on with our trek. Fact of the matter is, all I had to do was keep an eye on the trail and the horizon. Wash had taken to looking after his older brother, and Chance was taking as good a care of Asa as was possible, and not doing a bad job at it. I reckon he took that 'owing him one' piece of wordage he'd spoken the night before pretty seriously, for I could see he was in a good deal of discomfort at times himself. I never have been able to figure that out. A doctor takes a look at his patient and explains that the man might be in a little 'discomfort' from that gunshot wound he's suffered. Hell, man, pain is pain, especially to the fellow who is suffering the gunshot wound. You'd think those citified doctors were using the word discomfort because they couldn't stand the sound of the word pain! It's enough to make a body wonder.

At any rate, with my three riding partners looking after one another, I had free rein to keep my eye on the trail to our front, which was a real comfort in itself. It wasn't that I didn't trust to not seeing any more Comancheros, you understand. It was the fact that this was their land, their territory. Besides, I'd taken note of the supplies Margaret had sent along with us this morning, and we were running low on food. There might be one or two more meals of her roast beef left, but after that we'd be down to some bacon and what was out here on the open prairie.

On the other hand, things did start to look promising. We'd been on the trail a few days now and were heading toward the Canadian

River, which is up in an area they were calling the Panhandle. One of the things you pick up on real quick out here is the way Nature works. Just like a body won't survive long without water, neither will plant life. You might say it's part of the Law of Nature. If it comes down to it, there are cactus a man can drink from that are full of water in these desert areas. Store it like the humps in one of those Arabian camels, they do. So keeping an eye out for greenery in this land is just as important as keeping an eye cocked for the Comanch' or the Comanchero. The difference between the two, of course, is that one specie will save your life, while the other will take it.

Heading north toward the Canadian, I'd begun to notice that the greenery of the areas was beginning to show more and more. That was a good sign, for that meant that there was water nearby in abundance, and animals too. If there were animals about, why, our supper meal might not be far off at all. No sir. Could be just over the horizon. Of course, that could be a Comanch' wearing that feather you'd see instead of a wild turkey, so it paid to be cautious on the hunt. I never have tried eating meat off of a Comanch', although I hear those folks up in Donner Pass had a go at that kind of lifestyle back in '46. Turkey will be fine, thank you.

We rode pretty much in silence that day,

Wash too busy looking after Asa and Chance to want to palaver about much of anything, Asa and Chance doing the best they could to keep from voicing the pain of their wounds. Me, I found myself wondering just how we were going to get Asa's boys out of the jail at this Hogtown place. Hell, pulling a six-gun and charging hell for leather into the place was one method I didn't believe would work. It was fine for charging Comancheros and the Comanch' out in the middle of nowhere, for you had all sorts of room to maneuver in, but within the limits of a city, it wasn't going to work all that well. No, this would take a mite more in the line of planning, so I set about formulating some kind of plan as the day went on. I wasn't all that certain it would work, mind you, but then, folks have been experimenting in this land they called Frontier for the better part of a hundred years, and sometimes by guess and by God was the only way of seeing if a plan would work successfully.

I had more than one thing that began weighing a mite heavy on my mind. Ever since the start of the war, there had been the emergence in our land of what some folks were calling gunfighters. The term itself seemed kind of silly, if you asked me, for people have been fighting with guns and over guns ever since those Chinese fellows began toying with the elements that made up

61

gunpowder three or four centuries back. The world had been a bit more explosive ever since, if you get my drift. But since the war had started, I'd heard about men like Langford Peel and Colorado Johnny, who claimed to be fast with a gun and good at killing with it, most of what they killed being other human beings. Peel had wound up killing Colorado Johnny when their paths had crossed, back in '60 or '61, I disremember exactly. This was all up around that Virginia City strike in the Montana Territory, you understand, but that just goes to show how far a man's reputation can wander if given a chance. Peel, as I recall, got hung a couple of years back, again up Montana way. The trouble was that Peel and this Colorado Johnny weren't the only two men fast with a gun. Others had sprouted up like so many weeds, leaving me no doubt in my mind that we'd run into our share in this place called Hogtown. At least we wouldn't have Langford Peel and Colorado Johnny to worry about.

Another thing that worried me was the shape Chance was in. All of us, including Asa, knew that Asa Wilson was nowhere near being fast with a gun, although he wasn't afraid to use it, nor was he what you'd call inaccurate with it. Shooting at an upright man from a prone position can be a tricky bit of shooting if you think about it, but that's exactly what Asa had done the night before, when the Comancheros decided to deal a hand in death. They just hadn't counted on the payback involved. Chance, on the other hand, was proving to be not only good with that Colt's Army Model of his, but fast as well. Having that going for him was going to help out immensely when the bullets started flying in Hogtown, and I knew that at some time or another they would. Now, I was no expert on this fast-draw stuff, but it seemed to me that a body ought to be able to stand his ground on an even keel in a fight such as this. I didn't know how Chance felt about it, but I wasn't certain he'd be in all that good a shape to hold his own in Hogtown, what with the looks I'd seen on his face that day. Not that I'd ever hint as much to him, you understand I've got more sense and a lot more pride than that.

Of course, there was one promising thing about this whole difficulty, and that was the certain knowledge that we'd be going up against a bunch of amateurs. I say that because I've been around long enough to know that learning to do anything well takes a good deal of time and practice. I remembered spending upwards of a decade of my life trapping with the likes of Bridger and Carson and Fitzpatrick up in the Shinin' Mountains, and even at the end of that decade I was still being joshed about how much I had to learn yet. What I'd never liked admitting to myself—and never to anyone else!—was the sour fact that what they'd said about some things was right. It was the same way with being a Texas Ranger and then a town marshal, and I knew it would be the same with this United States Marshal's badge I now had. You didn't just pin a badge on and get to know the law overnight. No sir. You had to read up on the laws of the land, not to mention the laws that would concern the way you did your job in your area of responsibility, be it Texas or the town of Twin Rifles. A U.S. Marshal can travel just about any damn place he pleases in this land, or so I was given to understand, so I knew I had a hell of a lot of book reading to catch up on, a hell of a lot. The point is—and this made me rest a mite easier toward the end of the day—the same thing is true about learning to handle a firearm of any sort. You just ask Chance, he'll tell you. If Grandma said practice makes perfect, you can bet your bottom dollar she was right! The way I figured it, that put the three of us Carstons on the same ground with any of the vermin we'd be running into at Hogtown. No better, no worse. Me, I'll take those kind of odds any day.

We made the usual dry camp at noon that day, taking better care of the horses than us. Or maybe I should say I did. It was still

Wash taking care of his older brother, which still amazed Chance, and Chance looking after Asa Wilson, who seemed to be faring much better, although it was evident that he was still in a good deal of pain.

'You notice there are a good deal more leafy things appearing now?' I said to no one in particular.

'Yeah,' Wash said, nodding his head in agreement. 'Thought I seen a couple more jackrabbits than usual too. Maybe a prairie chicken to boot.'

That was about the extent of our conversation. Words tend to dry up quicker than an empty well in desert heat when a body has other things on his mind, I reckon. Like pain.

By late afternoon I'd pretty much thought out how we should approach this Hogtown business. Like I say, I was feeling a lot better about it too, having had the time to think like that.

What we'd ridden into by the time I was ready to call it a day was a valley of sorts. Compared to the desert area we'd been in these past few days, it seemed like paradise in bloom. There was a river running through it, and it was fringed with a good many willow trees and thick bushes. Like I said, plants will grow where there's water. It's as simple as that. Unless my eyes were going bad, there even looked to be a beaver or two in the area, for they had built a dam on part of the river and a creek that branched out from it. Mind you, it had been a long time since I'd been in this part of the country, but I'd wager that creek was Tascosa Creek. There were birds aplenty and wild game that ran to several members of the cat family, and we aren't talking kitty cats either. I also thought I'd seen signs of good-sized lobo wolves, coyotes, antelope, bear, and even an elk or two. By the time I'd chosen a campsite, I'd pulled out that Henry rifle of mine and shot a wild turkey for our evening meal. It wouldn't be as good as the kind Margaret could put together, fixings and all, but it would do for four hungry men at the end of a long hard day.

'There's plenty of water on that creek yonder,' I said to Asa and Chance while the turkey was cooking, 'so you can drink to your hearts' content. Cool water at that.'

'Fine,' Chance said in a voice that sounded gravelly from a long day of eating dust and heat. It hadn't gotten any cooler until day's end. I emptied the half-filled canteens and brought them back filled with cool water that the two all but gulped down, asking for more once they were through.

'You'd better save room for some turkey, Chance,' Wash said with a grin, 'or I'll eat the whole blame thing myself.' That brought a fiery look to Chance's eyes, which I took to be a good sign. At least the boy hadn't lost his appetite.

Asa and Chance ate with the same passion with which they'd drunk in that first canteen of cool, fresh water. I wasn't sure whether it was all that food that put them to sleep or the trek of the day, likely a combination of both, but within half an hour after they'd finished, they had gone to sleep.

'They held up pretty good today,' I said as Wash and I had a last cup of coffee that night. He nodded agreement. It was then I told him of my plans for entering Hogtown.

Tomorrow.

CHAPTER SEVEN

Wash was up early with me the next morning, although we let Asa and Chance get as much rest as they could. They'd need it. Besides, maybe a couple hours extra sleep here and there would help their bodies recuperate a mite quicker. Wash was good with a gun, but then, I'd made sure both my boys knew how to use both handgun and rifle by the time they'd hit double digits in their age. Still, it was Chance who was one of the best I'd seen with a firearm of any kind, although I doubted the day would ever come when I'd mention that thought to Wash. If there's one thing Wash had going for him, it was picking up on things real quick like.

'We're really gonna need him, aren't we?' Wash said in a matter-of-fact way as I finished putting a pot of coffee on the fire to boil. Maybe it was instinct in the boy, or maybe he'd seen the way I was looking at his brother just then; hell I don't know. But he'd pretty much picked the words out of my brain, that much was for sure.

I paused a moment, trying to think of some way to agree with him without hurting his feelings. After all, if he'd indeed read my mind, I was in a lot of trouble and had one hell of a lot of explaining to do to him. I tossed another piece of deadwood on the fire and stood to my full height. I was a full head taller than my youngest boy, and I wanted him to know it was his daddy talking to him now, not some trail rider he'd been with for the better part of a week.

'I don't know how it was in that war you boys were in, son,' I said, adding a stern touch to my voice and cocking an eyebrow at him, 'but I remember real well what it was like in the Mexican War.'

'How's that, Pa?'

'Well, you recall how it is at the start of a war, at the start of all wars,' I said with a chuckle before continuing. 'They get Old Glory out and wave her around, and them politicians speak big important words about how you boys are doing such a great job and we'll win this war in no time at all.'

'Ain't that the truth,' Wash said, smiling some as he dug back in the recesses of his own memory and found the exact instance I was talking about.

'But you know something, when we got off to the fighting area and the shooting started, why, those big-mouthed politicians were nowhere in sight! Hell, it was me and the friends I'd come to know who were doing the fighting. And what it come down to was the pure and simple fact that we had to count on one another to bring us through whatever battle or skirmish we were fighting. Yes sir. Wounded, dead or dying, we all knew we could count on the man who rode into battle with us, and knew he felt the same way.'

'I know what you mean,' Wash said with a nod. 'Ain't no tin-can shooting match. The bastards was shooting back at you with real live bullets.'

'Well, I ain't dead yet, so stop saying pretty words over me.' The sound came from the ground, in the form of a growl. Sure enough it was Chance.

'There now, you see,' I said to Wash, as though we'd been discussing something important. 'I told you if we started talking 'bout him, he'd come right to life.'

'Well, you got my attention,' Chance said, pushing his blanket back and taking his time to get to his feet, sloshing his hat on and rubbing his eyes as he did so.

'Don't use that word attention to me this early in the morning, boys,' Asa said, now also coming to life. 'I'm too goddamn old to try getting this body in any kind of a straight line anymore.' He even chuckled when he'd finished remembering his old army days, so I knew he was getting better, a whole lot better.

'After about the first year,' Chance said, 'I was pretty much wanting to get those battles and the whole damn war over with, so I could come home.'

'You actually spent time thinking about coming home, coming back here?' I asked in an incredulous manner. It seemed I was continually finding out all sorts of new things about my boys.

'Hell yes,' Chance said with a grin. 'Had two reasons in mind.'

'Do tell.'

'First off,' he said, looking at his younger brother, 'I wanted to beat the living hell outta you.' All three of us Carstons knew he had done exactly that, for that was how I found my boys the day they both rode back into Twin Rifles from the war. Fighting like hell, just like the boys I remembered raising. Turning only slightly to face me, he added, 'And I wanted to show you I could do it by myself and come back alive to boot.'

I smiled at both of them, feeling a short moment of pride in them, as mad as they'd made me when they stomped off to war. 'Well, you boys seem to have done a fine job of going off and coming back, ary you ask me,' I said.

When Asa and Chance came back from the stream and throwing some water on their faces, Wash was in the middle of his meal of bacon and biscuits and I was dishing some of the same up for them. Once they all had food in their mouths, I said my piece, figuring it might be the only way I'd get a word in edgewise with these three in my presence.

'I never did get to finish what I was saying.' I paused, taking a sip of my coffee. 'What I was telling you about the Mexican War of mine, Wash, well, I said it for a purpose. The fact of the matter is we're all four gonna have to be counting on one another when we ride into this Hogtown place. If we don't do that, we ain't gonna be much more than memories to the Ferris and Porter women in Twin Rifles.'

I spoke my next words directly toward my two boys. 'There ain't gonna be no room for bickering like you two are known to do. We're gonna have to get in this place and do some checking on Asa's boys, get 'em out and get the hell out of this place. Much as I like the greenery and the water up here, I got a notion I'm not gonna be too keen about

71

the clientele in this town.'

'I get your drift, Pa,' Chance said with half a mouthful of food. 'By the way, Wash, thanks for helping out yesterday, I really appreciated it.' He was about to take another bite of his food when he stopped, a thought hitting him in the form of an idea, and smiled. 'In fact, you did such a good job, I'm gonna let you get my horse for me again this morning.'

'You wish,' was Wash's reply. So much for brotherly love.

I could tell Chance had gotten a lot better too, for he was back to his old self, griping like hell when he saddled his mount, although he did a credible job of it for a man with a hitch in his gitalong. I ought to know, for I've got a mite of a limp my own self. War wound and all that; good for a story or two about my days in the Mexican War. Normally, I used a knotted-up old cane to help me along, but had forsaken the cane on this long trip. Besides, it would likely just get in the way.

Asa wanted to saddle his own horse, but Chance was right there to do it for him. And did he gripe about that? Not on your life, not a whisper's worth! I swear it was a miracle seeing the difference in the two sides of my oldest boy that morning, going from one extreme to another—from straightforward, down-right direct and mean, to humble as a church mouse. Why, you'd think there was something wrong with the boy's mind!

I'll give Asa Wilson this much. As soon as he heard me talk about how we'd likely be riding into Hogtown sometime today, he started acting like he'd never been shot at all. He'd checked his loads on his Colts and Henry like it was nothing out of the ordinary, but I had a notion the boys knew as well as I did that he was still in a good deal more pain, at least in that upper right shoulder, than he was willing to let on. I knew Chance in particular would be knowing how that felt, for the lad had been shot in the upper portion of his body more than once since returning from the war. I'd been shot more than once my own self in the past fifty-some years, so I knew it was no fun at all. Still, Asa put up a brave front, no matter how he was feeling. I reckon that's something else you pick up on in raising kids. On my worst day, I'd never really let on to my boys how badly I was feeling.

The horses and Otis had gotten their fill of the grass in the area when we'd made camp the night before, appreciating it almost as much as we did, I believe. They had a whole lot better disposition about them when we broke camp that morning, sort of like the men who rode them, you might say. It's amazing how a decent meal will make a body feel like facing the world all over again. It purely does. Of course, I also pointed out to the boys and Asa that we were down to next to nothing and in need of supplies once we got to Hogtown, and that getting Jeremiah and Thomas out of jail wasn't going to be our only business in town.

The sun had only been up an hour and a half, maybe two at the most, when we came within sight of what must have been Hogtown. All we needed was Asa's nod to know that it was. I doubted the man would ever forget the place.

From a distance it didn't look any bigger than Twin Rifles. But I'd found out a long time ago that towns are a good bit like people, it's hard to tell about them by their looks. They can be big and tough or small and quiet or anywhere in between. The ones I'd taken a caution to were the quiet ones, no matter what their size. The quiet ones can be hell on wheels if you aren't careful. Like I said, they're a mite like people, these towns.

While we were pulled up to a halt and taking in the outskirts of this place called Hogtown, I took to pinning my marshal's badge on the way it was supposed to be worn. Chance gave me a hard look and frowned.

'You sure you want to do that, Pa?' he said. 'Seems to me pinning that badge on is an instant invite to lead poisoning.'

'Well, son, I always figured that lead

74

poisoning is part of the job description,' I replied, trying to be philosophical about the whole matter. 'On the other hand, if I'm worth wearing this badge, I reckon this is the place to find out for sure.'

Little else was said about the matter, and we all took to rechecking our loads again. Not that any of us were afraid, you understand. Cautious was more like it. Besides, I'd seen too many handguns fail a man because he wasn't overly cautious about making sure they worked right. No sir. None of us were afraid. At least, none of us was going to admit it then and there.

It was Wash, Asa, and me who rode into Hogtown right slow, the three of us abreast. Chance was the one who brought up the rear. I reckon that military life he'd been living for the last four years had conditioned him to be aware of more than one type of ambush. Fact of the matter is, both of them were thinking that way, I'd reckon. While Chance was keeping an eye on the streets, his brother was watching the rooftops, or what there were of them.

By the position of the sun, I'd gauged it to be somewhere around half past eight, which accounted for the fact that the town still looked like it was half asleep. Oh, there were a couple dozen people on the streets all right, but they didn't look like any businessman I'd ever see going to open his general store or the bank. They looked downright mean to me, and made no pretense of showing it to the four of us. If that was supposed to scare me, it didn't.

We got a pretty good look at the false fronts and tents and the dozen or so permanent buildings that had been established as we made our way down the main street. I'd noticed on the way in that there were a few houses on the outskirts of town, but not many. On first sight, Hogtown gave the impression of being a rather new town. It was just that the people in it tended to look like old customers. If you get my drift.

Any man worth his salt is going to take care of his horse before he takes care of himself. You cuss them and kick them and sit on their backs while you expect them to do the hard work of the day, so you'd better take care of them proper or some day they'll throw you flat on your keister. The livery was at the far side of town, so we got a good look at the place as we rode through town.

A young lad of fifteen or so was pitching hay about as I dismounted in front of the livery. 'Can I do anything for you, sir?' he promptly asked. He was attentive enough, I'll give him that.

'Matter of fact you can,' I said, sticking my hand out in greeting. He took it without a word, giving back nothing more than what appeared to be an honest smile. 'We just come a far piece and these horses are plum tuckered, not to mention Otis there,' I added, pointing to our pack mule. 'What'll it cost to get 'em all a good feed and a rubdown? We'll be here a day or two, give the mounts a chance to rest up afore we resupply and move on.'

The boy took us all in and did some mental figuring for a moment. When he was satisfied, he said, 'Four dollars for two days for the lot of 'em.' He was trying to sound businesslike in his manner, and I found myself respecting the boy for it. It seemed rather obvious from where I stood that the livery wasn't doing an awful lot of business at the moment.

'That's fine, son,' I said, and began fishing around in my pocket. When I came up with a five-dollar piece, I plunked it down in his hand. 'That ought to take care of the whole shebang. You take good care of 'em and you've made yourself a profit to boot,' I added with a wink.

'Hold it!' I suddenly heard Chance say in a commanding voice to my rear. By the time I turned around, I could see he had his Colts out and trained dead on someone, and that someone was trying to gather up the reins to Otis. Whoever the yahoo was, he never had a chance.

By the time I'd pulled my Remington and

was making my way around the side of the mounts, the would-be thief had already sealed his fate. Wash was still atop his mount and had his own six-gun leveled at the thief, not to mention Asa and Chance. But he had guts, I'll give him that. Or he was desperate.

'And who's gonna stop me?' he said defiantly, tugging as hard as he could, despite the fact that there were at least three guns pointed at him.

Chance had taken three steps toward the man by now and used his momentum to advantage. With six-gun still in his right hand, he swung his left hard and made a bone-crushing contact with the side of the man's head. If Chance hit as mean as he looked sometimes—and he did—the man should have been close to dying by the time he hit the ground.

'Smart ass,' he growled as he grabbed the reins from the man's hand. 'Where's your local law?' Chance asked the boy at the livery.

'He ought to be up the street in his office,' the boy said in a civil tone that was leaning toward the edgy side. 'You passed it on the way in.'

Chance grabbed the man by the scruff of the neck until he was on his feet and half dragged him toward the boardwalk that would lead him to the jail. Asa accompanied him.

'My name's David,' the boy said in a more pleasant tone. David Farnsworth.' I looked at the sign above the livery that read Farnsworth's Livery.

'Your daddy run this, son?'

A sad look came across his face as he said, 'Used to. He's ... Now it's just me.'

I bet a dollar he was about to say his father was dead. After all, this was Hogtown, and if it lived up to its reputation, it would only seem natural that the boy's father had died here by lead poisoning more than a natural death.

'That's a lot of responsibility, David,' I said. 'But you look like you handle it well.' I scratched the back of my neck, as though to remember something. Real serious like, I added, 'You just make sure that all my supplies and rigging are on the animals when I leave here, just like they are now.'

The sadness turned to fire and the boy stood a mite taller as he spoke. 'You wouldn't be accusing me of stealing, would you?'

'No, son,' I said with a smile. 'It's just that I've got a list of all the supplies I'm supposed to have, you see.'

'What he's saying, son,' Wash said in a half-joking voice, 'is that when he gets through with his list, he'd better have all of his supplies or you'll wind up going on the bottom of that list. And son,' he added, shaking his head, 'you *don't* want to be on any list he's carrying.'

CHAPTER EIGHT

Wash and I caught up with Asa and Chance about the time they were fixing to enter the city marshal's office. Chance was still madder than hell, so I told him to let me handle the situation. Besides, I was the fellow wearing the U.S. Marshal's badge. Both of us knew that I likely had more patience than Chance would ever have in his entire lifetime, so that aspect wasn't discussed at all.

Entering the lawman's office, I could see that it wasn't much bigger than mine back in Twin Rifles. It had been my experience that most lawmen shared about the same abode when it came to office space. An oversized desk with two or three chairs were scattered throughout the office, a potbellied stove with a coffeepot atop it, a bulletin board of sorts with a few wanted posters, and at least one rifle rack and a couple of holding cells. That was what most of us had in one form or another, and it didn't look like it varied much for the marshal of Hogtown.

The man seated behind the desk looked to be a different matter. Rising to his feet as we entered, I could see he was at least my size, maybe outweighing me by twenty pounds. He might have had twenty pounds on me, but I had a good twenty years on him. It was just the gray creeping into his black hair that gave him a touch of maturity, as Mother once put it. There were crow's-feet around his eyes and a couple of lines running across his forehead indicating he'd known worry and a few hard times. His eyes had a weary look to them, a faded brown that first off gave me a questioning look. I reckon it was seeing my badge that changed any doubts he might have had in his mind.

'Howdy, marshal,' he said with a cautious smile, extending what I took to be a friendly hand once I got close enough.

'Howdy,' I said, returning the smile and the handshake with the same caution it was given. 'Name's Will Carston.'

'Nice to meet you.' The words came out formal, as though he'd say as much to any stranger simply to be courteous. Not that I could blame the man, for indeed I was a stranger in his town. 'Ray Dunston here.'

'Seems you got some light-fingered people in your town who don't rightly care who knows it,' I said, tossing a thumb over my shoulder at Chance and the would-be thief he had in his iron grip.

'Yeah, that's Garrick, all right,' the marshal said, more annoyed by the man he set his sights on than anything else. 'What'd he do this time?' he said, moving out from behind his desk, the keys to a cell in his hand.

'He tried awful hard to take an old pack mule of ours,' Chance said in his best level voice. I could tell he was feeling a strain about it, for it just didn't seem natural to him. But then, this wasn't a Comanchero he was dealing with, but a man with a badge. 'Seems damn near as hard-headed as the mule.'

'Oh, he tries,' Dunston said with a half smile. 'Keeps wanting to prove he's tough as some of the yahoos come into this town. Truth is, he's got mush for brains and hardly no sand at all. But he tries running a good bluff.'

Ray Dunston grabbed a shoulder full of shirt and guided Garrick toward a cell down a short hallway with two or three cells on each side. This was one aspect I found to be a might different than the office I had back in Twin Rifles. I had two side-by-side cells and hardly anyone in them at any given time. The marshal of Hogtown, on the other hand, seemed to be doing a fair amount of business from the looks of it. He was just throwing Garrick in a cell when I saw Jeremiah and Thomas Wilson in the cell at the end of the hallway. Asa saw his children the same time I did, and Dunston saw Asa about then.

'Not you again,' the marshal muttered as the old man moved by him toward his sons.

'I told you I'd be back,' Asa was saying to his boys in a matter of seconds. If those bars hadn't separated them, they'd have been hugging one another, they were that close. If hugging was a sign of closeness, I couldn't say that I'd done much of it with my own sons, in recent years, at least.

Chance and Wash laid their six-guns on the marshal's desk and quickly made their way back to the Wilson boys and their cell, catching up on old times and anything else they could think to talk about. It had been some time since they'd seen one another, the Wilson boys having gone off to war too.

Back at his desk, Ray Dunston offered me a seat and a cup of coffee, offering to lace it with his own brand of bottled whiskey. Once I saw the bottle actually had a brand on it and wasn't some of that homemade poison, I let him pour a dab in the hot liquid and thanked him for it.

'Just how did those Wilson boys get put behind bars, Ray?' I asked, hoping a first-name basis might make him more talkative. I also added the fact that Asa Wilson was a friend of mine and asked me to look into the matter in an official capacity.

He mulled it over real careful, taking a sip of his coffee as he did, and I got the impression that the only reason he was

83

passing any information on to me was because I was wearing a federal lawman's badge. It's kind of hard to resist answering questions put by a man wearing that particular badge, I was finding.

'It was a couple of Thad Wayne's boys who brought 'em in,' he said almost hesitantly. 'Thad Wayne himself filed charges against 'em. Murder it was. Killed Homer Abb.' Homer Abb, as it turned out, was one of the clerks in the local bank, although I had to admit that it surprised me that this town actually had a bank, as rowdy as it appeared to be from its reputation. The killing was also supposed to have taken place in the evening and under the cover of darkness. When the marshal got through talking, the thing that stuck in my craw was the fact that there didn't appear to be any eye witness to the killing, and the only reason the Wilsons were in jail was on this Thad Wayne's word.

'And just who is this Thad Wayne?' I asked, finishing my coffee. The whiskey had added a good deal of flavor to the coal-black coffee.

'Thad Wayne is the head of the city council. You could say he has a good deal of influence in Hogtown,' the marshal added as an afterthought.

'You mean he runs the place.' I said. There are times I have as little tact as

Chance, but I try to limit them.

Dunston shrugged. 'You could say that.' I noted that he didn't put an awful lot of pride in the words he spoke. Fact of the matter is, I was getting a real narrowed-down feeling that Ray Dunston wanted to run this town the way it was supposed to be, but wasn't being given the chance. I was willing to bet a dollar that this Thad Wayne was behind it all too.

'Well, thanks for the coffee, Ray,' I said, setting the cup down and standing up. 'Thanks for the rest too.'

Asa, Wash, and Chance came out from the back cells and silently retrieved their sidearms. But I could tell by the hard looks Asa and Dunston were giving one another that the two had a silent war of some sort going on between them.

'I'll be outside in a minute, boys,' I said to them. 'Why don't you see if you can spot an eatery sign, and we'll see if we can't make up for that slim breakfast we et this morning.'

'Sounds good to me,' Chance said. The thought of a meal always sounded good to that boy.

When Asa and the boys had left, I turned to Ray Dunston.

'There is one other thing, marshal,' I said, speaking to him in both an official and a personal capacity.

'What's that?'

'Asa Wilson was damn near dead when he came riding back into Twin Rifles. I don't suppose you'd have any idea of how he got that way? I'd hate to think you had anything to do with it,' I said, my voice picking up a slightly harsh tone.

'Carston, there ain't no way I'm a crooked lawman, if that's what you're thinking,' he said, all hospitality gone from his manner now. 'There's some hard men in this town, all right, but I won't be bullied by any of them. You just ask around, if you don't believe that.'

'I'll do that,' I said, letting the man know I'd do just as I said. I was at the door when I stopped and turned to face him one last time. 'And Asa Wilson?'

'From what I understand, he had a run-in with a couple of Thad Wayne's boys.'

'I see.'

'Listen, Will,' the man said, calling me by my first name for the first time, 'you watch your backside when you're around Thad Wayne.'

'I'll do that, Ray. Thanks.' Then I left.

CHAPTER NINE

Reed's Café claimed to have the best food in town and lived up to their brag for the most part. They served up a better than average plate of ham and eggs, although their cook would have to go some to come anywhere close to Margaret Ferris or John Porter's establishments, not to mention their cooking. Naturally, Chance put the food away like it was his last meal and he was the condemned man. Asa did most of the talking during that meal, wanting to know over and over again how we were going to get his boys out of jail.

'I'm studying on it, Asa, I'm studying on it,' I kept reassuring the man. One thing was for sure, as distressed as he was over his sons and their difficulty, he hadn't lost his appetite one bit. No sir. Put away damn near as much food as Chance, he did. I took that as a good sign that the man was healing properly.

'What now, Pa?' Wash asked outside the café. It's a good thing he wasn't talking to his brother, for all he'd have gotten in reply was a belch.

'This Thad Wayne character is starting to intrigue me,' I said.

'What have you got in mind, Will?' Asa asked, still waiting for some pearl of wisdom on how his boys were going to be set free.

'Well, Asa, truth to tell, I'm thinking we need to get two things done at one time, not intending on being here that long,' I said, hoping he'd take that as a positive sign that I

87

hadn't completely forgotten about his boys. When he smiled and nodded, I hoped my prayers had been answered and he'd quit pestering me. Any more of his anxious behavior and he'd really get on my nerves. 'Let's take a walk over to the general store and see what they have to offer in the way of supplies.'

Grant's General Store seemed like a ticklish type of name to carry in a land this far south, especially since the war hadn't been over that long. Still, you took your supplies and such where you could find them. Used to be you had to go to a big-time city or a trading post to get your supplies, but since the fur trade had closed down and all those people had begun moving west, why, these newfangled stores were showing up in damn near every town that opened up. They carried a variety of materials, from dresses to guns to seeds for the field to hard rock candy. Asa picked up a new shirt and Chance a new pair of pants. When it came time to shell out the money, I asked the proprietor, a bearded man of middle age, what he knew about Thad Wayne.

'Why do you ask?' were the first words out of his mouth. He was suddenly as guarded and cautious as the marshal had been. Thad Wayne was apparently a touchy subject to get people to open up about in Hogtown.

I pulled my jacket back some to let him see

the U.S. Deputy Marshal's badge. 'Let's just say it's official business and leave it at that,' I said. When he still didn't answer, I added, 'Ain't none of us gonna hurt you, if that's your worry.'

'Shoot, man, those are my boys they've got locked up over there,' Asa said in a testy voice, an arm shooting out in the direction of the jail. No sir, he didn't seem lacking in energy now at all.

The man looked carefully about, as though spies were eavesdropping on his every word. It wasn't until I saw the bruise on his neck that I could understand his suspiciousness.

'Can't be too careful,' the man said in a whisper.

'You the Grant on the door's name?' I asked. I dislike talking to a body with no name. Tends to make me a mite suspicious my own self.

'Yeah. Zeke Grant.' No offer of a handshake or a welcome of any sort, just a name.

'You were saying,' said Chance. I had a notion he was wanting to know about Thad Wayne as much as Asa and me.

'He's the head of the city council in Hogtown.'

'So I've heard,' I said. 'You know anything else about him that'll make that sound like old news?'

After a good deal of thought, Grant said, 'He runs this town. Got his own brand of outlaws that do his bidding for him.'

In a way, that was news. I'd suspicioned from the start that Thad Wayne kept the lid on this town. But it wasn't until Ray Dunston had mentioned that Asa had gotten beaten up by some of Wayne's men that I got the inkling that this town boss was running anything but an honest game. Now I had one of the town's merchants verifying it for me.

'How do you know these are outlaws that he's got working for him?' I asked. I'd seen a lot of people make accusations about someone else over the smallest of things and call them anything from a thief to a killer in the process. Some people like to embellish on the truth, if you get my drift. But I had a notion that the man standing before me now had pinned the right moniker on Thad Wayne's associates. I just wanted to hear him say so himself.

A deep frown came to his face as he leaned across the counter and, in a harsh voice, said, 'Mister, for about a year now, those sonsabitches have been coming in here on a monthly basis and helping themselves to the proceeds of my work. I call that stealing, at best.' He spit the words out like so much soap in his mouth.

'You mean protection money,' Wash said.

'The correct term is extortion,' I said,

knowing exactly what both were referring to. 'Is it just you? Or are there others?' I asked.

'Nearly every merchant in town is in the same pickle,' Grant said, his voice suddenly forlorn.

'Well, why don't you fight back?' Asa asked in an incredulous manner.

'Why don't we fight back? I'll tell you why, old timer,' Grant said, poking a finger at Asa. 'Thad Wayne made it real clear that if we don't cooperate in *his* town, he'd do some cutting and shooting on our families. And damn near every businessman in town has got a family. You don't believe me, you just ask young David down at the livery. It was his daddy tried bucking Wayne not long ago.'

'I see,' I said, and I did. Killing David Farnsworth's father had sent a message to the community, and they had all taken heart. After all, no one wants to die, nor see their family members killed.

'Am I getting old or just senile?' Asa said in a flustered voice. To the storekeeper he added, 'I thought I said my boys were being held in your city jail. Now, mister, do you think they're just having themselves a Sunday social behind them bars? Hell, no! Why, I'm surprised they ain't tried to hang 'em yet!'

'What are you getting at, old-timer?'

'Would you believe it, Will, the man's

91

blind as well!' Asa blurted out.

'Blind!' Grant said in an equally offensive voice.

'Why sure! Didn't you see the badge on his chest, mister? That's a marshal's badge, by God! A *United States Deputy Marshal* at that!' Grant was still dumbfounded, still confused by Asa's words. 'Ask him! Ask him for some help! I did. Why do you think I'm here? Sure ain't for my health!'

'Couldn't hurt, mister,' Wash said before Grant had a chance to make a reply. 'Why, I hear these federal lawmen can do some powerful things, Yes sir.' Leave it to Wash to stretch the truth.

'That true?' Grant wanted to know, not that I could blame him. Hell, I'd want to know just what kind of odds I was playing against too if I was walking into the lion's den with nothing more than a slingshot.

'In a manner of speaking,' I said, although I'll admit it is often hard to sound confident when using those particular words. More often than not, it sounds like you're running a bluff, and at the moment that was exactly what I was doing. Hell, I hadn't cracked any books on these federal laws; there hadn't been time. Until I found some of those fancy federal law books, I figured I'd use the same horse sense that I'd used all along when I'd pinned on a badge, be it Texas Ranger, city marshal, or this newfangled federal man's badge. I'll never forget Mama reading to us youngsters and impressing upon us the importance of two documents that we were always to know. One was the Good Book and the other was the Constitution. I'd always figured using them made up the law of the land, in a way.

'What is it you got in mind, lawman?'

'Well, it's like this, Grant,' I said, trying to think as fast as I was talking. Finally I settled on telling him the truth. Most times the truth is how it's going to be anyway, so you might as well face up to it. 'I originally come here to get Asa's boys out of jail on some trumped-up charge.' I didn't want to hurt the man's feelings, for he surely did appear to be in a fix of his own. But all of a sudden I wasn't sure how to break it to him, wasn't sure at all if the advice I was about to give him was any good. Real quick I was getting this notion that the federal law was a lot more complicated than the simple law of the land I knew, and that can scare a body, especially someone new to it.

'Now it seems that your hard times are becoming part of the Wilson boys' affair,' Chance said. 'Me and Pa was talking it over just this morning, and we figure this Thad Wayne is likely behind putting the Wilson boys behind bars. But you see, Grant, it's a matter of first things first.' The boy never ceased to amaze me! Not that I was sure of the truth of everything Chance had just said, you understand. But he sure had pulled my fat out of the fire.

'That's right, first things first,' I said, trying to sound more confident.

'There now, didn't I tell you,' Wash said with a nod of encouragement. 'The man can do powerful things. Yes sir, powerful things.'

Grant apparently felt much more convinced about our ability to help him out of his predicament. He rubbed a callused hand across his beard and gave me a thoughtful look. 'I'll tell you what, mister. If you want proof of what I've been telling you, you stop by here at closing time. I'm expecting Wayne's men to stop by for their monthly protection money.'

'Well now, that sounds right interesting,' I said, and made it a point to be at Grant's General Store at least an hour before closing.

CHAPTER TEN

The town was coming to life as we left Grant's General Store. I heard some shouting from inside a saloon across the street and next heard and saw a man come tumbling through the bat-wing doors, fall and roll across the boardwalk into the dusty street.

'Looks like the owner's getting rid of yesterday's trash,' I said.

Asa chuckled. 'That or the drunks are coming to life.'

Zeke Grant had given me the name and location of the town doctor. I'd seen a grimace on Chance's face, and thought it best to hunt up the local physician and have the professional take a look at my doctoring methods. I never did claim to be any sort of a fix-up man, at least not more than temporary.

A. GRIZZARD, PHYSICIAN is what the sign on the side of the building said. An arrow underneath the sign indicated a flight of stairs up to a second-story entry. I took note that the doctor's office was only two buildings down from the jail.

Doctor A. Grizzard was an older man, likely my age or a mite older, although I'd never take to anyone calling me an older man. A man's got his pride, you know. He was clean-shaven in an era when full-grown beards and mustaches were what those fancy back East folks called in vogue. I'd seen more than my share of those Matthew Brady pictures of men in uniform, young and old, wearing some kind of beard while they stuck their hand inside their uniform. You'd have thought they all took lessons from Napoleon on how to stand for a picture. Foolishness. The doctor, at any rate, took enough pride in

95

himself to shave on a daily basis. I thought I saw my squint in his eyes, although I couldn't picture myself wearing a clean white shirt and string tie every day. he also sported a vest like one of those river-rat gamblers will wear. He was tucking a pair of spectacles in his vest pocket when we walked into his office. He had the same kind of iron-gray hair I did, and was a good foot shorter than me. Still, I did see a bit of myself in the man. Maybe I was getting a mite old. Maybe pride wasn't something that mattered anymore.

'Got two customers for you, Doc,' I said.

'I can see you have,' he said, quickly taking in the makeshift bandages Chance and Asa were sporting. He was just a mite on the blunt side, if you ask me. I never did get along with those types, but held myself in check for the moment. Maybe this man could give us a bit more information on Thad Wayne and the situation in Hogtown. It was doctors and bartenders, after all, who heard just about the worst that anyone had to offer.

He directed Asa to a room off to the side to examine him. In five minutes he was back, silently searching for something in his glass cabinet. I'd never seen so many cutting tools that looked so small, but I was also wagering that they were a hell of a lot sharper than the bowie knives any of us were carrying. Hell, it was a doctor's way.

'Who treated this man?' the doctor asked in another ten minutes, reappearing from the examining room. He didn't look or sound any too happy about the words he spoke either.

'I did.' The badge I wore didn't seem to impress him, even when he took a glance at it.

'You sure aren't a doctor, mister,' he said.

'Hell, I know that! Thing is, I saved Asa's life,' I said with a nod of assurance.

The doctor gave me a low sounding 'Harrumph.' I reckon it gave him time to pull a frown over his face as he continued. 'It's a good thing you got him to me when you did. That wound of his is about to fester if it isn't treated right,' he said in a low voice, throwing a thumb over his shoulder at the room to his rear.

'Don't you worry, Doc, ol' Asa's tough as can be,' Wash said. 'He'll make it. Why, he come into our town with a couple of bruised ribs near a week ago, and he's still going.'

'That's another thing,' the good doctor continued, pointing a stout finger at my youngest son as though it were all his fault. 'Those aren't just bruises, young man. Your friend has likely got a couple of cracked ribs and needs to be resting. If he's not careful, he's going to have internal bleeding of one type of another.' He stopped spouting off a minute and ran a thick hand across his face, the way a man will who is tired, or maybe just tired of seeing the things a doctor does. When he spoke next, the tone of his voice had changed, although it was still Wash he was talking to. 'Your friend Asa may be putting on a good front, son,' he said in a soft, gentle voice, 'but every movement he's making is giving him pain. And son, no man is that tough.'

The startling realization that I'd been as wrong about Asa and his health as I had made me feel quite ashamed of what I'd done to the man. Had I only made him worse in pulling the bullet out of him? I certainly hoped not.

'I guess you're right,' I said in a low voice, suddenly feeling like the child who has been severely reprimanded when he thought he'd done something right. 'I'm no doctor.'

'Look, friend, I know you saved his life, and that's good,' the man said in a more understanding voice. 'But he's got a ways to go before he'll be doing any speedy recovering. Now, I'll bandage his ribs good and tight, and I've got some salve to put on that wound to keep it from getting infected, but you boys are going to have to make sure he does more sitting than walking if you want him to get better.'

'You've got a deal, Doc,' Wash said with an enthusiastic grin, speaking for all of us. I reckon if there was one way of letting the doctor know that Asa Wilson meant a lot to us, Wash's words had said it all.

'You make sure and check with me in another day or so, and I'll change the bandage and apply some more of that salve,' Doc Grizzard said. 'He's not out of the woods yet.'

The good doctor applied more of his salve to Chance's wound, which was far less critical in nature than Asa's. Chance was advised to stay off his feet as much as possible, in order for the wound to heal properly.

'How much?' I asked, when the two were ready to leave.

'Two bits each.'

I fished around in my pocket and plunked down a dollar on the man's desk. 'Better hang on to this as advance payment, Doc,' I said with a half smile. I was starting to take a liking to the old cuss.

'Advance payment?' he said in a look of puzzlement. 'You plan on needing my services soon, do you?' It was looking at my badge again that brought to his mind what I had said and why. 'Oh, I see.'

It was then I told the doctor my story about Asa and his boys and the trouble we'd run into with Thad Wayne, including how we'd uncovered the trouble he'd been making for the merchants and their families in Hogtown. Chance and Asa had taken seats while I spun my tale, Wash remaining in a standing position and gazing out the window. Doctor A. Grizzard had proceeded to clean his hands in a washbasin and listen to me at the same time.

'You've got teeth, marshal, I'll give you that,' he said when I was through speaking. With the first smile I'd seen him make since we'd walked in, he added, 'I don't know how long you'll have them, mind you, but you've got teeth.' I could only assume this was the doctor's way of saying I had courage.

'My biggest problem so far has been trying to find out about Thad Wayne,' I said, wondering if this would be the man who would fill me in on the horrors of the man running Hogtown. 'People seem awful scared of him hereabouts. Don't much want to talk about him at all.'

'You're right about that, marshal—'

'Why don't you call me Will. Will Carston's the name.' Like I said, I was taking a liking to the old cuss.

'Well, Will, he's got most all of this town buffaloed.'

'*Most* all the town?' Chance said frowning. 'Who isn't buffaloed?'

'Me, for one.'

'You?' I reckon Chance didn't figure this old man for much of a fighter, but like I said, you never can tell.

'Certainly me.' Doc Grizzard was getting

100

real persistent all of a sudden. He blinked the way a man will who has a nervous tic, and smiled. 'Told old Faraday I'd put buckshot in his ass and refuse to take it out if he tried any of his tactics on me.' He winked knowingly at Chance. 'Stayed away from me too, he has.'

'Who's Faraday?' I asked. I had a notion a piece of this puzzle was about to fall into place.

'He's the chief henchman for that band of thieves.' Doc Grizzard didn't seem to be worried about hurting anyone's feelings when it came to talking about Thad Wayne and his bunch.

'You don't seem to be afraid of them.' I wasn't going to say it, but by God, he reminded me of me!

'Hell, no! Threats don't scare me anymore,' he said with a good deal of finality. 'Why, I'm pushing seventy! Do you think after what I've seen, I'm going to be *afraid* anymore?' I knew just how he felt.

'You said there were some others who won't take any guff from Wayne?'

'Well, yes and no,' he said reluctantly. It was as if he wasn't sure, more than being afraid of anything or anyone.

'Yes and no?'

'Yes. I know for sure Davy Farnsworth will kill any of them who give him a hard time,' he said. 'That fifteen-year-old down at the livery?' Chance said in an awestruck voice. Obviously, he had temporarily forgotten some of the manly things he had done at the tender age of fifteen.

'He's sixteen, and don't let his young looks fool you,' Doc said, pointing a finger at Chance. 'In case you hadn't heard, they killed his father not long back. Davy's about to turn into a man real soon. You mark my words. He's going to surprise a whole lot of people around here.'

'Who else?' I said.

'Well, there's Ray Dunston, but I've got my doubts about him.'

'How so?'

'It's like this, Will. I think he's got the courage.'

Once again Doc Grizzard ran a tired hand over his face. 'I just don't think he has the will or desire to stand up for this town anymore.'

'How's that?'

'You mean he's like a man looking for a woman to call his own and make a go of it with,' Chance said.

'Sir?' Doc frowned.

'He wants someone who'll stand beside him, not behind him.'

Doc raised his eyebrows in astonishment. 'Crude but to the point, young man. Yes, I'd say that's it exactly.'

'I wonder what it'll take to get your

marshal believing in the townspeople again?' Chance said, wondering out loud. 'Or what it'll take to get the people believing in the marshal?'

Chance's words almost knocked me over. Usually, he'd been muttering or making some smart-ass remark, so talking in complete sentences seemed like a minor miracle.

'Well, I'm real pleased, Chance, real pleased,' I said.

'Pa?'

'Why, making such a philosophical comment.' I turned to leave. 'I think it's about time we picked up those supplies from Grant's and take 'em back to the livery.'

'Pa? What are you talking about?'

In as straight a face as I could muster, I said, 'There may be hope for you yet.'

'Wash, what the hell is he talking about?'

'Let it be, Chance,' Wash said. 'You'll never understand it.'

Out of the corner of my eye I thought I saw Doc Grizzard trying to stifle a laugh as we left.

CHAPTER ELEVEN

Of all the supplies I'd ordered at Grant's, the only things we'd taken with us to Doc

Grizzard's were the shirt and pants Asa and Chance had purchased. They'd changed into those when the good doctor had applied his salve and fixings along with a good amount of bandages. The rest of the supplies I'd ordered were things Grant had in bulk in the rear of his store that would have to be repacked on Otis before we left. Zeke Grant had adequately packed the supplies in two boxes, which he loaned to us with the promise that we'd return them once we'd finished packing Otis. Wash and I convinced Asa that we were the healthier of the four of us and would carry the boxes down to the livery. Chance didn't make a fuss about getting out of doing something his brother could do in his place, which didn't surprise me at all.

It was walking over to the livery with a box on my shoulder that I noticed it was starting to heat up as the sun moved toward high noon. I also took to worrying about Asa Wilson and what Doc Grizzard had said about him. I had paid careful attention to the fact that Asa had done more coughing than usual since leaving the good doctor's office. Was it from the bandages Doc had bound him in? Or did he give Asa an elixir of some sort that he didn't tell us about? I knew for a fact that many a doctor had medicines that tasted more like poison or some kind of homemade brew than anything else, and that some of those potions were as hard to stomach as a bartender's homemade whiskey. Or had Doc Grizzard been right when he said that Asa was indeed a sick man needing to slow down? Was he dying before my eyes and me not knowing it? Worse yet, had I been the one responsible for the condition he was now stuck with? I had all those questions and more going through my mind as we walked to the livery.

A body ought never be allowed to think when there was as much going on around as there had been for us since riding into Hogtown. If I hadn't been distracted by all of those questions, I'd have seen what was going on at the livery before Chance did. I'd have gotten rid of that box I was carrying and gone to young Davy Farnsworth's rescue before Chance did, and Chance wasn't really in any condition to fight, any more than Asa, at least according to Doc Grizzard.

I found myself wishing that Doc was there, for he wouldn't believe what was happening. Talk about tough! While Wash and I still had those boxes on our shoulders, Asa and Chance lit into the two men who were holding Davy Farnsworth back by the arms while a third one took to softening up his gut with one hard blow after another. The boy was about to turn blue and lose whatever it was he'd last eaten, when Chance grabbed one of the toughs holding back Davy and

105

threw him aside like some rag doll. The man turned around in a circle twice before falling to the ground amidst Wash and me. I'd set my box of supplies down on some hay off to the side of the entrance of the livery. But it was Wash who was the quick thinker.

The man Chance had thrown our way landed right on his back at Wash's feet. My youngest didn't waste any time—he dropped his box of supplies right on the man's stomach. Now, hoss, that box had to weigh as much as mine, and that was a good forty pounds, lest I miss my guess, so this fellow wasn't going anywhere quick.

'Stay,' Wash said, as though talking to some mangy cur dog he was tired of tangling with. When this supposed tough started moving his hand toward his six-gun, Wash stepped on the hand and growled, 'I said stay.'

At the same time Chance was pulling one man off of Davy, Asa took to the same chore on the boy's other side, quite successfully too, I might add. In fact, he made me feel a whole lot better when I saw him do what he did. Mind you, Asa wasn't as strong as my oldest boy, but like I say, you just can't tell about people and the way they look. In Asa's case, it was determination more than strength that got the job done. He knew good and well the man he was going to tangle with was bigger than he, so Asa simply played by the other man's rules and stuck a foot out behind him when he pulled him back. The man tripped, landing flat on his ass. By the time he was moving to get up, Asa had pulled out his pistol and laid it up alongside the man's head, settling him back down on the ground in a permanent fashion, if you get my drift.

Once those two toughs weren't so tough anymore, that left the one beating on Davy's stomach to face Davy all by himself. As it turned out, he wasn't all that tough either. Oh, he was big, all right. No doubt about it. But Davy was mad, and I do believe he'd reached a turning point. While the man beating on him was looking about to see where his friends had gone, Davy brought the flat of both hands up alongside the man's ears, which resulted in a startled look coming to the big man's face. Davy's actions had given him enough time to react, and that was just what he did. He hit the man hard, twice in the face, once with each fist. By that time I'd moved around to the man's rear and caught him when he staggered into me as a result of Davy's fists. I grabbed one shoulder and turned the bastard around to face me. Then I hit him in the gut, and hit him and hit him and hit him some more in the same place, until all I had to do was watch him drop in his own breakfast.

'Sorry ass,' I mumbled as I stood there

over him. It was apparent by now that no one was going to do anything, for Chance, Asa, and Wash all had their guns out and were just itching for a fight of some type, if anyone would oblige them. A crowd was gathering, and I'd no doubt some of them were friends of these sorry excuses for men who now lay on the ground, but they didn't want to buy into this game, not on a bet.

'You look like a good man to have for a friend, marshal,' young Davy Farnsworth said, stepping forward. Even though he was feeling his side gingerly for damage to his ribs, he had a smile on his face. But then, the winners usually never do feel the pain as much as the losers in these types of fights. Believe me, I know what I'm talking about, friend, for I've been on both sides of a good fistfight. Trouble is, I never had seen much good come of any of them yet.

'Doc Grizzard was right,' I said, taking his handshake. 'You are a surprising young man.' He smiled at the compliment. But the smile was short-lived when I pointed out that he was also bleeding from the mouth some. He undid his neckerchief and started dabbing at the side of his mouth.

'Less'n you got horses to pick up or turn in, I'd get to moving along, folks,' Chance said in a growl that was meant to sound harder than it was. When no one moved immediately, he brought his Colts up level

108

with the crowd and cocked it. That got their attention real quick. Jogged their memory too, I reckon, for they all found someplace else to tend to their business.

'Chance, why don't you and Asa take these yahoos over to the jail and tell Dunston I'd like 'em locked up,' I said.

Chance nodded. 'I'll tell him Mr Farnsworth will be down to file charges on 'em shortly.' I wasn't sure whether Chance was trying to sound like some knowledgeable lawman or trying to make the boy before me feel better, but I had a notion he was accomplishing both. Busted-up ribs and mouth or not, David Farnsworth had just been treated like an honest-to-God man, and the first time that happens in a body's life, well, it's really something. You know what I mean.

'What was you doing to bring those three vultures down on you?' Wash asked when the crowd had dispersed and we were pretty much alone. 'Sassing 'em or something?'

The boy planted his hands on his hips and took a serious stance before us, as though ready to fight all over again if need be. 'You know, mister,' he said in a tone meant to be hard for a boy his age, 'with all due respect, I never have been able to figure out just where you draw the line. What's the difference between you mouthing off and me sassing someone? Ain't nothing but the difference in our ages, if you ask me.'

The boy was right, of course. When a boy mouthed off, he was sassing, while when a man did it, he was what I call a smart ass. Boys you spanked or gave hell. A grown man you ignored or gave hell to, usually in a different form than the way you approached a boy. Still, Davy Farnsworth was right.

'Well, I reckon you've got a point there, Davy,' I said. 'And, truth to tell, a young lad going into manhood, like you are, can get right confused about all of it. I think what you want to remember, son, is that having a big mouth don't make a big man, not in this land or any other.' I gave him a wink and a nod. 'Guaranteed.'

Wash smiled. 'That's right, Davy. Next time you see Chance, you ask him about what Pa says.' Wash looked at me and smiled again in a knowing way. 'You just ask him.' I'd made a comment similar to what I'd just told Davy to Chance not long after he'd returned from the war, which didn't seem all that long ago, when I thought about it.

'I'll do that,' the boy agreed.

'Now then, you were saying about how this difficulty came about,' I said.

'Oh, yeah.' Davy paused for a moment, taking in a gulp of air before he continued. What he told Wash and me was the same story Zeke Grant had told us earlier that morning, all about the collection practices of Thad Wayne and his henchmen. 'I reckon they started early with me, figuring I'd give in to 'em.'

He was silent then, and I could see that he had pulled back within himself, for whatever reason I wasn't really sure. I could see by the look about him that being a man didn't matter so much anymore, for there was something terrible inside that had his total attention now, and it bothered him something fierce. I don't know how long Wash and I just stood there, waiting for him to speak, but after a while I thought I knew what it was that had grabbed hold of him and wouldn't let go.

'You know, son, if I was a betting man, I'd bet a dollar that your daddy got killed doing the same thing you were doing just now,' I said in a gentle tone. If I was right and his daddy's death was on his mind, the boy was in a fragile state of mind. If it was anything like the way I'd felt about Cora, then I knew exactly how he was feeling.

'You'd win a dollar, marshal,' Davy said with a sniffle. If I hadn't seen him act like such a grown-up man a few minutes back, I would have taken him in my arms, remembering more than once that I'd done that to my own boys when they were at the tender age of fifteen. You'd just never hear them admit to any such emotion. It wasn't something a man was supposed to be accustomed to doing. Instead, I placed a firm, steady hand on his shoulder, the way I remembered an old-timer doing to me once in my youth in the Shinin' Mountains. The gesture was one that was supposed to indicate a transference of strength from one man to another. I thought Davy knew what it meant too.

'I'm sorry to hear about your pa, Davy,' Wash said, and I knew he meant the words. Like I say, Wash is a bit more compassionate than his brother.

'Pa was on the city council too, you know,' Davy said, talking like a real man would, holding back his emotions, no matter how much of his guts they were eating away. 'He wasn't a merchant like most of the rest, but he was an honest man, which is likely why they elected him to the council. But he never did like Thad Wayne, and liked his tactics even less.' He stopped here to take in another lungful of air. When he took his kerchief and dabbed at the side of his mouth, I also saw him run it across his upper lip under his nose and didn't say a thing about it to him. Like I said, a man's got to have his pride, and Davy Farnsworth had definitely earned it, in my opinion. 'It was the day after he challenged Thad Wayne at a council meeting, told him he'd take Wayne to the marshal, that Pa got killed.' The next words came out fast, as though they had to come out that way or they would never be said. 'Shot him dead and stuck a pitchfork in his chest. Left him right here in the livery, they did.' An arm shot out like a bolt, pointing to a spot near the center of the big building. 'Right there they left him.'

'Who did it?' I asked.

'Wayne and his men.'

'Why didn't Marshal Dunston do something about it?' I asked.

'Yeah, I heard he didn't take any guff from Thad Wayne,' Wash added.

'Nobody saw him do it,' David said, 'but I *know* it was Wayne, I just know it! The marshal said there was no proof.'

'Can't fault Dunston for that,' I said, feeling sorry for the boy.

'Wasn't much he could do, I reckon,' Wash said in agreement.

'So these yahoos figured you for an easy touch, that it?' I said.

'I reckon.'

'Seems to me you showed 'em how it's done,' I said.

'I don't know,' the boy said in a modest way, 'I doubt I could have lasted much longer if you folks hadn't come along.'

'Don't you doubt it for a minute, son,' I said with a nod. 'I seen the look in your eyes, and that was mad, son. You take my word for it, mad will get you out of a fix more times than anything else you can think of.' Indeed it would, for it was the same kind of mad—or should I say madness—that I'd seen in Chance's eyes a time or two. I knew for a fact that it was as dangerous as a rattlesnake at a gopher convention. But rather than tell Davy Farnsworth that, I thought I'd let him find out for himself. His day would come.

'Well,' I said, pulling out my pocket watch and taking note of the time, 'what do you say we stop by the marshal's office and file that charge?'

'Yeah,' Wash added. 'You want to make sure these yahoos spend a while behind bars.'

CHAPTER TWELVE

When Davy filed the charges against the three men who had assaulted him, it was a surprise to find that the man who had been beating the hell out of him was Faraday himself, Thad Wayne's chief honcho. I reckon I should have expected that, for Davy had said that they had been making their rounds early that day to collect extortion money, and unless I was older than I thought, Doc Grizzard had said it was Faraday who'd come around threatening him on the same matter.

Ray Dunston seemed to take a bit of pleasure in putting the three men behind bars, especially when he saw the shape they were in, which was none too good. 'I can't recall having this many men in these cells in some time,' he said as he filled out the paperwork for Davy to sign. He wasn't grinning from ear to ear or anything like that, you understand, but I had a notion he wasn't sorry to see Faraday and his men behind bars either. A lawman can tell, especially when he's dealing with another lawman.

'Well, Pa, I don't know about the rest of the town,' Chance said when we left the marshal's office, 'but that marshal just got the hell impressed out of the way *we* handled something in this town.'

Chance was right, and I said as much to him.

*   *   *

'Now all we've got to do is convince the man that all but two of those prisoners belong in his jail,' Asa Wilson added, as though to remind me in his own subtle way that his boys were still in the Hogtown jail. The trouble was Asa Wilson was about as subtle as a bull in a china shop. If you get my drift.

I pulled out that pocket watch of mine

115

and, noticing it was high noon, suggested we find a saloon and wet our whistles. All three of my companions were for that, and within five minutes we'd found one of the half-dozen drinking establishments in Hogtown.

The nice thing about some saloons is that they'll leave what they were calling a free lunch on the bar for patrons who'll order a drink with their meal. If you were one of the drunks who was simply trying to fill his stomach until he could cadge money for another drink, you could forget a free lunch. This was for paying customers only, which meant, if you thought about it, that it wasn't really a free lunch after all. The four of us eased our way into the saloon, which had once been called the Red Dog, the sign having long since been shot full of holes, and made our way to the plate full of half-cut sandwiches.

'Beers all around, ary you've got them, barkeep,' I said in my most welcome voice and smile. I remember Daddy telling me before I left home that if I could order a drink and cuss in the language of the country, I could likely get along pretty well there. He'd also cautioned us that there were only three people we'd have to smile at in our lifetimes, they being the bartender you ordered your drink from, the woman who was variously cooking or serving food to you, and the fellow standing across from you when he had the drop on you. I'd spent the better part of my life smiling at Cora, who had cooked and served some of the best meals I'd ever eaten in my life. Like the present situation I'd done my best to smile at the man serving up my drinks. As for that last one, well, hoss, I never have gotten used to smiling at some fellow holding a pistol of sorts on me. No sir. Mostly, it was killing I had on my mind then.

Asa and my boys had grabbed up a handful of those sandwiches. Me, I was doing some thinking on what was happening to the people in this town. When the barkeep set down four beers that looked to be slightly cool but not ice cold, I remembered that the town doctors and bartenders were almost as good at getting information from as the town gossip. Maybe this man behind the bar could shed a little more light on what I'd need to know about Thad Wayne and Hogtown.

'Say, friend,' I said, tossing a coin on the bar top, 'I understand old Thad Wayne pretty much runs things hereabouts.'

'Mister,' he said in a serious tone as he surveyed the coin I'd just given him the way an old miner would when he was looking for the real thing, 'if you don't know it by now, I guarantee you'll know it before you leave.'

'Well, now, that sounds right threatening.' I was more curious than shaking in my boots, for I'm a mite like old Doc Grizzard in that I don't scare too awful easy. 'You want to tell me how that'll come to pass?'

He disappeared, pouring a half-dozen drinks before returning to where I was perched. 'Word's getting around pretty fast about what you fellas and that Farnsworth boy did to Faraday. He ain't used to people bucking him.'

I shrugged. 'People change,' I said, 'sometimes for the better, I hear.'

'Not Faraday. He's pretty much used to having his way.'

'What happens when he doesn't get his way?'

'Let's put it this way, friend,' the barkeep said in a voice as serious as the plague. 'He's got plenty of friends, and there's at least five of 'em sitting at that table over there.' He nodded toward a table directly to my rear as I faced him. Beer in hand, I slowly turned to face them, smiling as though they were old friends. I raised the beer to them, smiled again, and turned back to face the barkeep just as slowly as I'd turned around.

'Grovelly sort of bunch, ain't they?' I said. Except for one youngster who appeared to be a mite younger than Wash, the rest looked like drifters who were down on their luck, or flat didn't know how to dress. Aside from that, they looked awful dirty. The only thing they had going for them was the fact that they looked awful mean. But like I said, I don't put much stock in looks.

'They'll do anything Thad Wayne tells 'em to, mister, and right now they've got the four of you on their minds.'

The young lad at the table was the first one to make a move. He wore a clean-looking work shirt, and trousers that were just as new. The only thing that looked old about him was the dusty pair of boots he wore and the pistol and cross-draw holster he sported. His hat hadn't been out in the sun long enough to fade or get a sweat stain. If you took the gun off of him, he looked as though he was dressed for a Sunday social. But the six-gun changed all that, and there wasn't anything peaceful about him now as he approached the bar.

Asa was on my left. Wash was closest to me on the right, Chance right next to him. I knew they'd heard my conversation with the barkeep and were aware of what was going on, or what might go on, take your pick. The young upstart pushed his way in between Chance and another drinker at the bar. Without ordering, he turned to Chance.

'I'm Johnny Warren,' the young man said, as though bragging about it.

'Bully for you, son,' Chance said, only briefly glancing at the man on his right. If the boy's name was supposed to mean something to Chance, it surely didn't. For that matter, I didn't recognize the name either. Be that as it may, this young man was on the prod, and it was Chance he was out to get.

'Hey,' he said, pushing Chance hard on the forearm and causing his beer to spill on the bar top. 'I understand you busted up my friend's chest this morning.'

Before Chance could reply, it was his brother who decided to step in. Wash stepped away from the bar so he was in full view of this Johnny Warren character. 'I'm afraid you've got that a mite wrong, friend. Actually, Chance just tossed the fella around a mite. I'm the one who near busted up his chest.' The way he was talking, you'd think he was discussing today's weather. Some days that boy is hard to figure.

John Warren totally ignored Wash, keeping his hateful gaze on Chance. 'Don't matter, friend,' he said. 'This is the one I want.'

Chance turned around and looked Warren full in the face as though the man were out of his mind.

'You don't really want to do this, do you?' Chance said. 'I just come in here for a beer, and now you jump off of your toadstool and start getting froggy.'

'Don't worry, mister,' the boy said with a leer, 'I'll make it fair.' He then proceeded to lift his six-gun out of his holster and lay it on the bar to his right. 'Put your gun on the bar and we'll see who can get to their gun first. What could be fairer than that?'

I was fast getting the idea that this was one of those young lads who was wanting to become another Langford Peel. If he was as much a beginner as anyone else, that meant Chance had an even chance of beating the man. But as Chance took the Colt out of his left holster and placed it on the bar top next to Johnny Warren's, I also remembered that those two shots Chance had taken since returning from the war were both in his left shoulder. If I remembered correctly, that arm was slow to heal from that second wound, hadn't completely healed yet. That put Chance at a disadvantage, but if it did, he didn't seem to notice it. I swear, both of these boys were hard to figure out at times!

I took about three steps out and away from the bar and the line of fire these two combatants would cause, placing myself about a foot behind and a foot to the right of Wash, who was repositioned just about that same distance behind his brother. I couldn't see Asa, who was now to my rear somewhere.

Patience is not a virtue of the young. Chance simply stood there and gave this would-be gunman some hard stares that only seemed to make the lad angrier. Johnny Warren was waiting for Chance to make a go for his gun, likely because he figured he was faster than Chance at this game. The two of them couldn't have been more than five feet apart.

When it came, I couldn't believe my eyes!

Quick as a cat hunting a cornered mouse, Chance had him. Oh, Johnny Warren was good with a gun, all right, he was fast. But it was Chance who outmaneuvered him. For Chance, it was eye and hand coordination that was on his side. Chance did three things at once when Johnny Warren grabbed for his gun. His left hand reached out and batted away Warren's gun, causing it to fire wild when he got a hold of it. At the same time, Chance had also taken one step closer, just to make sure he'd be within range to knock the man's gun away. The third thing he did was draw that Colt from his right-hand holster and shoot Johnny Warren in the right shoulder, bringing about both a look of pain and surprise as the young man fell to the floor.

While Chance and Johnny Warren were having their shootout, Wash and I got our guns out, just in case the rest of the these yahoos were wanting to ante up this hand. I do believe that if Wash and Chance ever had to go head to head with their pistols, they'd likely kill one another. I was thankful that would never come about. Wash had his gun out before me—maybe I was getting a mite old—and stuck it in the ribs of one of the men nearest him, who was trying to get out of his chair and pull a gun at the same time.

'Don't!' he said in a firm, hard voice. 'Unless, of course, you want to die in that position.'

The man stopped, plunking himself back down in his seat. He knew he was beat.

By the time I had my Remington out, I'd taken enough steps so I was able to stick it right in the throat of another man at the table who was trying to do the same thing—kill me. He stopped dead in his tracks when he felt that barrel in his neck and heard me cocking my six-gun. I'll guarantee that's got to be one of the loudest noises in the world, especially when the gun is pointing at you.

'Do you know that your chances of seeing the sun set today are somewhere between nil and next to nothing?' I said, poking that gun barrel just a mite harder into his throat. You'd have thought the man had lost his voice, as quiet as he got all of a sudden. Or maybe he had. The kind of position he'd gotten himself into will do that to a body sometimes.

'Barkeep!' I heard Asa yell out behind me. Not moving the position of my Remington one bit, I looked over my shoulder. There was Asa, six-gun out, cocked and ready to shoot the barkeep. Of course, the barkeep

123

had a hand somewhere under the bar too. 'You bring up anything but a beer in that hand, and you'll die regretting it.' The barkeep's hand came away real nervous like, settling on top of the rag he was wiping the bar with. The only other thing he had was a sheepish smile.

It was about this time that Marshal Ray Dunston came bursting through the doors, gun in hand. He had an anxious look about him that clearly said he'd shoot the first one who gave him any backtalk.

'All right, what's goin on?' he said, looking the situation over.

I didn't know what to say, for it was Chance who had taken up the gunfight, even if this Johnny Warren had pushed for it. After all, the Good Book says it takes a bigger man to walk away from a fight than to head straight into one. But then, the fellow who wrote that up never did come on the likes of Chance Carston. Chance managed to surprise me again by coming up with a pretty logical explanation.

Seeing the marshal with his gun still out, Chance holstered both of his guns. 'It's like this, marshal,' he said. 'This young Dan'l Boone comes up to me at the bar and starts pushing for a fight.'

'So far I believe you,' Dunston said when he saw Johnny Warren laying on the floor, a look of pain about him. 'This kid ain't

124

nothing but trouble.'

Chance continued, telling the marshal how Warren had challenged him and laid his gun on the bar, encouraging Chance to do the same, all in the name of fairness. 'He was the one who went for his gun first, marshal.'

'He cheated!' Warren yelled, his words coming out in pure pain. 'He pulled his gun and shot me, for God's sake!'

'That true?' Dunston wanted to know.

'Hell, yes!' Chance said. 'He said go for your gun, and I did. Mind you now, marshal, I never did play this game, laying your gun down on a bar. So I went for my gun, and if I hadn't, he would have killed me.'

Dunston shook his head in disbelief, running the story through his mind as he did. Then a crooked smile came to his lips and he glanced at Johnny Warren. 'Looks like you got beat at your own game, son. I'm calling it self-defense. The man went for his gun, just like you told him to. Best thing you can do is get that wound looked at and get out of town. And Warren? Don't come back to Hogtown.'

Johnny Warren's friends gathered around him and started helping him out of the saloon. But Ray Dunston wasn't through speaking to this crowd, and he made sure they all heard what he had to say.

'You know, folks, I told Marshal Carston we had a real friendly town here,' he began.

'Now, I know that sometimes people get crazy and get into fights. But maybe you'll want to keep something in mind. I understand they don't take a liking to getting their kind shot.'

'What kind's that?' one man asked, trying to be sarcastic.

'*United States Marshals*,' Dunston said, putting particular emphasis on those three words. 'I understand they hang 'em high and fast.'

I do believe walking out of that saloon was the quietest I'd heard that establishment all day.

CHAPTER THIRTEEN

We spent the rest of the afternoon verifying what Zeke Grant and Davy Farnsworth had told us about the extortion attempts by Thad Wayne's men. Once we convinced the merchants that we were on their side and were looking out for their best interests, they opened up to us with a good deal of relief. It's amazing how much of their hard times folks will tell you once they find out you're on the law's side. Mostly, they were just plain scared for their lives, for many of them had sons who had gone off to war and, in some cases, had yet to come back. In a way,

126

you couldn't blame them for backing down to Wayne's thugs, for they were fighting the odds—something like a dozen to one in most instances—with nothing but an early death and a cold grave to look forward to. No sir, you couldn't blame them at all.

'You know, boys, I've got a notion that the days of men like Thad Wayne are about over,' I said when we stopped in at Reed's Café for supper late that afternoon. What with that trouble in the saloon, I hadn't gotten much in the line of food, and was feeling a mite more hungry than the rest of our group, which is saying something when you consider Chance's appetite. It had been my decision to eat early, especially if we were going to be meeting the likes of Thad Wayne's bunch. Naturally, Chance was right there to second the motion.

'How's that, Will?' Asa asked when we were through ordering from the bill of fare. The young lady we gave our order to was a pretty young thing, all right, but my boys seemed a whole lot more interested in their menus than in taking her sights. If I needed any kind of confirmation that Chance and Wash had a serious interest in Rachel and Sarah Ann back in Twin Rifles, I reckon sitting there in Reed's Café was it.

'Well, Asa, the way I see it, our boys are coming back from this damn war they were off to,' I said with a firm nod, 'and right or wrong, those who are making it back are gonna be plenty experienced in surviving.'

'True,' Asa said, taking a sip of coffee.

'Why, I seen right off a difference in my boys when they come back. Mind you, they could pretty well take care of themselves before they left. It was when they come back that I noticed that they wasn't gonna put up with any more pushing around, less'n of course they was the ones doing the pushing.'

'I noticed,' Asa said with a smile, giving the boys a side glance as he did.

'That's right, Pa,' Wash said, taking part in the conversation now, 'there ain't gonna be no *boys* that come back from this war. None who's gonna take kindly to being called a boy, anyway.'

'A body gets shot at and missed and shot at and hit all too often—sometimes in the same day—to be called a boy anymore,' Chance added. 'Boys may be the ones going off to wars, but I can guarantee you it's the men who come back from 'em.'

'Got that right,' Asa said in a firm voice, likely remembering his own days in the Mexican War, just like me.

'That's what I'm getting at,' I said, taking the occasion to get my say in before everyone else took to yammering again. 'Once the fathers and sons get back from this war, it's gonna be tougher than hell for men like this Thad Wayne character to keep any kind of grip on a town like this, or any other one, for that matter. I tell you, people just won't stand for it!'

All three murmured assent, and we ceased any palavering while the food came, paying more attention to it than anything else in the café. We'd each ordered a beef steak with fried potatoes and biscuits and as much coffee as they could refill our cups with for the meal that afternoon. There must be something about eating your own cooking that makes a body attack a piece of home-cooked beef like it's trying to get away, for I spent upwards of fifteen minutes making that meat disappear. I must have really been involved in that food too, for I didn't recall hearing anyone enter the café after we did, and we were the first customers the place looked to have that afternoon. But then I had my back to the door too. Or maybe I'm just getting old.

I had to shake my head twice when I heard the short, sharp scream, knowing right away that it could come from no one but the young lady who had waited on us. Then I thought I heard old Doc Grizzard's voice.

'Hear now, you let her go!' he said.

When I looked over my shoulder, Doc was getting up from his seat near the front of the café. Apparently, he'd walked in some time after us and taken a seat by himself. What he was so riled about was a man who had taken hold of the waitress's arm as she stood at Doc's table. There was still steam coming up from Doc's plate, so I could only assume that she had just laid his meal before him when this plug ugly came in and grabbed her arm. Remember now, Doc was a mite to the small size, while the man he was facing had a good deal of heft to him. Yes sir.

'Please, Jeff, you heard him,' she said in a distressful tone, 'let go of me. You're hurting my arm.' She was about to start crying if the sound of her voice was any indication. Evidently she knew this fellow from someplace, and common sense told me to stay out of it. But I never have gotten used to seeing a woman—any woman—hurt by a bullying man.

Like I said, I must be getting old. By the time I made the decision to get up and do something about the situation, several things had already taken place. Doc Grizzard had made an attempt to free the man's grasp from the girl and gotten pushed back into his chair for his efforts. The young girl didn't like Jeff's hold much and had stuck her pencil down into the fleshy webbing in between the thumb and forefinger of the hand holding her arm. It must have been a sharp pencil, for Jeff—or whoever the hell he was—let out a cry of his own, mixed in with an oath or two.

And Chance was already on his way to

saving the girl.

He'd taken about two big strides toward the man by the time I was out of my seat, and by then he had one hand firmly grasping the man called Jeff, tearing it loose from the girl's arm.

'Sonny, you just interrupted a meal I been looking forward to all day,' Chance said in a hard, even voice. He'd let go of the girl's arm, but still had a tight fist around Jeff's wrist. I noticed he was pressing his thumb down the right side of the man's wrist, bringing about a fair amount of pain by doing it too.

'That was a mistake, mister,' Jeff said in a growl that didn't sound quite real. But then men who take to beating up on women are usually like that when they face one of their own breed.

'Say, Jeff,' I heard Doc say next. He'd gotten up again and was standing off to the man's left. I saw Doc shift his weight some and, when Jeff turned to face him, hit the bully square on the nose. Jeff's look changed from one of toughness to one of surprise as he put his free had up over his nose, but nothing could stop the gush of blood that now came flowing from it. 'Smart-alecky kid,' Doc grumbled as he massaged his fist.

'What the hell—' The gruff-sounding voice came from a man in an apron that was once white but now looked soiled and dirty.

He wasn't all that big, but he had a good-sized cleaver in his hand and looked as though he could use it. He'd appeared from what I took to be the kitchen area, and I was betting he was the girl's father. Once he saw that his girl was unharmed, he stood there for a moment and took the whole scene in as it played out.

'You'd better find a doctor, sonny, or you're gonna bleed to death,' Doc said.

'You can take a look at me Doc, can't you?' Jeff said, almost in a whiny manner now.

'Me? Of course not,' he said stubbornly, as though the pure consideration of the question was an absurdity. He sat back down and picked up his knife and fork. 'Why, can't you see, I'm eating supper.'

'Open the door, Mr Reed,' Chance said, and grabbed Jeff by the scruff of the neck. Reed did as Chance asked, and Jeff was soon rolling out across the boardwalk and into the dusty street. He landed right at the feet of Marshal Dunston.

'You oughta get that nose taken care of, son,' Dunston said in what seemed to be a sincere piece of advice. 'You look like you're gonna bleed to death.' Then he stepped around the bloody man and entered the café.

'I wonder what that was all about?' I said matter-of-factly as I took my seat again and stuck a now cold piece of beef in my mouth.

Dunston pulled a chair from a nearby table, turned it around and sat on it between Chance and me. He was good at making himself at home.

'If he was giving Carrie a hard time, it's likely because the boy doesn't know how to handle women,' Dunston said with a smile. 'For about six months now she's been turning him down, and he's been getting forceful about it.' The lawman looked over his shoulder toward the kitchen area. 'Some day I expect old Herschel is gonna put a stop to that boy's interfering on a permanent basis.'

'I know what you mean,' Wash said. 'I saw the size of that cleaver.'

'I imagine you got a reason for just pulling up a chair at our table, marshal,' Chance said, stuffing the last of his own plate of food in his mouth. 'Or did you just know it was time for our after-dinner coffee and figured on joining us?' The edge had come back to Chance's voice. But then you couldn't blame him, not when you had feelings as strong about hot food as Chance did.

'As a matter of fact, I'm just paying a professional courtesy,' Dunston said in reply, a touch of ice to his own voice now. He started to say he could use some coffee, but Carrie beat him to it, plunking a cup down before him and filling it with the hot black stuff.

133

'I want to thank you men for helping me out,' she said in an awkward way. It was easy to see she was getting embarrassed over Jeff and his actions. 'I'm afraid Jeff isn't much on manners around women.'

'Guess I'll have to set him down and tell him all my worldly experiences with women,' Chance said trying to smile and be polite as he spoke. 'Why, you'd think he was trying to be some kind of ladies' man or something. Me, I put an end to that right quick!'

'Don't you worry, ma'am,' I said, giving her a wink. 'Chance sits down to talk about his worldly experiences with women, why, it ain't gonna take but a minute.'

Asa, Wash, and Dunston laughed at my comment, as well as the girl, although in the girl's case I had a notion it was more out of relief that she was laughing than anything else.

'By the way,' she said as she readied to leave our table, 'Papa says not to worry about the meal. He says you more than earned it. Once again I want to thank you for helping me out.'

Then she was gone.

'Now then, Ray, what's this professional courtesy you're talking about?' I asked, finishing off the rest of my meal.

'It's Faraday and his cellmates. They're on the loose,' Dunston said, suddenly quite serious about the subject he was talking about. I got the very distinct idea that there was little love lost between Faraday and Dunston.

'How'd that happen?' I asked in a frown.

'Apparently, Thad Wayne came over while I was getting some supplies and just took the men out of their cells.'

How do you know that?' Asa asked.

'It was your boys that told me about it. They seen it all.' Something in the back of my mind was telling me that I'd be able to count on Ray Dunston when the walls came tumbling down. He'd had Asa Wilson's boys in his jail for upwards of two weeks now, but I'd yet to hear him complain about how bad they were or how they'd tried to break jail. If they were dog-mean killers, I know that I sure wouldn't trust them. But Dunston didn't seem to hesitate about believing what they'd said about Faraday and his cohorts being released.

'You know why they're out, don't you?' Asa said to me.

'Yup,' I replied and pulled out my pocket watch. It was getting close to five-thirty. 'I do believe it's about time we pay a visit to Grant's store.'

'Yeah, I gotta git going too,' Dunston said, pushing the chair away from him. 'Just thought I'd pass that news about Faraday to you.'

'Well thanks, marshal, I appreciate it.'

135

In five minutes we were at Zeke Grant's store.

There was maybe an hour and some worth of light before Old Sol disappeared for the day, and it was fast approaching six o'clock. The customers had pretty much gotten what they'd come for today and were gone, all except for a frail-looking old woman who continually kept looking things over. She'd feel the cloth of the material and hold a dress up to her to see if it would fit, like most women would. But she never really had the look of a woman who was about to purchase something. And if she had a husband to do the purchasing for her, I sure didn't see him.

'Just who is that woman?' I finally asked Grant. Asa, Wash, and Chance had taken up various positions in the store, supposedly looking over the merchandise like any good customer would, like this woman seemed to be doing. Chance, of course, had immediately found the gun rack and took to going over the rifles, shotguns, and pistols Grant had available.

'That's Geraldine,' the store owner said with a chuckle. You'd have thought it was some kind of personal joke, and as it turned out, it was, sort of.

'Sure does do a lot of looking.'

Grant chuckled again. 'That's all Geraldine does. Believe it or not, she's the town gossip. Spends most of her days putting in a little time here and a little time there in the stores, making the rounds of nearly all of them in a day's time. Usually depends on how much gossip she picks up in the store.'

'Makes this her last stop, does she?'

'Why, of course I do!' The tiny woman's frail-sounding voice was in high pitch. 'I heard that, young man,' she added as she approached me, wagging a finger up and down. 'Yes, I did.' The closer she got, the more I could see that she was in her seventies or older, but she sure did get around for her age. Not a hobble or a limp of any kind, just those stooped shoulders you'll see in a woman of her years. And, apparently, ears that could pick up the conversation across the room without even looking at the people doing the conversing. 'I'm Zeke Grant's best customer,' she added when she'd reached the counter I was leaning on.

'Is that a fact?' I said in what was meant to sound like pure wonder. 'That true, Grant?'

'Actually, it is,' he replied with a smile. 'Geraldine picks up enough around town so she's more reliable than the newspaper, and comes around a lot more often.' I reckon everyone's got to be good at something, and Geraldine seemed to have a talent for picking up bits and pieces of information about town. From the way she was smiling, I was sure that she took a lot of pride in that fact.

Then something crossed my mind that got me a mite worried, and I found myself doing some quick thinking.

'Well now, Miss Geraldine, if you're that good, I reckon you've heard just about everything that me and Zeke been talking about since I walked in, is that right?' I said, hoping I was wrong as I spoke.

'Every word,' Geraldine said with a confident smile. What had got me worried was the fact that I'd spoken to Zeke Grant about how we figured to proceed to catch this Faraday pilgrim in the act and put him away. If this old woman had heard that and didn't exactly like the look of my face ... 'Oh, don't worry, marshal,' she added, still smiling, 'I ain't gonna tell your secret to Faraday or Thad Wayne. Shoot, I hate both of 'em as much as anyone else in this town.'

I don't mind telling you I breathed a sigh of relief, and didn't care who saw it or what they said about it right then. No sir.

'Tell me something, Miss Geraldine,' I said, rubbing a hand across my jaw in thought, 'have you ever done any work with the law?'

In a serious tone she said, 'No, I don't believe so. Not that I don't believe in the law, you understand, for I do. Most definitely.'

'Well, ma'am,' I said in my most conspiratorial voice, 'I've got a job I do

138

believe you could help me and my deputies with.'

'Really?' She probably hadn't been this overjoyed in a good twenty years, if I gauged the look on her face correctly.

'That's a fact, ma'am. Now, first off, I want you to stay out of the way when these yahoos come in and the trouble starts. I don't want a valuable person like yourself getting hurt none.'

'You can count on me, marshal.' She could have been twelve years old and entrusted with her first important duty in life, the way she said those words. Young at heart again she was.

'Good, Geraldine,' I said with an appreciative smile, and patted her on the shoulder. 'We'll talk about the other stuff I want you to do later,' I gave her a confident wink to show I had faith in her, and she went back to looking over the women's things in the store, acting as though nothing had happened.

I took up a stance just inside the alley entrance to the rear of the store, which wasn't very far from the counter. In fact, the only thing standing between the counter and me was the rack full of guns that Chance was gandering at.

I'll say one thing for Faraday—he was punctual. It was just about six o'clock on the dot when he came marching into Grant's

General Store, three of his men in tow. He stopped at the counter, reached into his pocket and produced a little book, thumbing through it until he apparently found the listing for Grant's store.

'All right, Grant, I've got you down for a hundred dollars a month,' Faraday said in a gruff voice that sounded just as mean as I pictured it to be.

Telling a man to stand there and be brave is a whole lot different than actually doing the deed. Grant swallowed hard and said, 'No, not this month.'

'What!' Faraday exploded. 'You mean you ain't got it?'

'No, sir. I ain't giving it.'

As I expected, it was Faraday who started the ball. He easily reached over, grabbed the shirtfront of Zeke Grant and slapped him hard across the face, drawing a small river of blood from the man's mouth.

'You stop that, Faraday!' Geraldine said, and was soon making her way toward the injured storekeeper. 'You've got no reason to hit Zeke like that.'

'Aw, shut up, you old bitch,' one of the henchmen said as she approached the counter, and with no effort pushed the frail woman back sending her sprawling to the floor.

That was when the man made his mistake. He must have been wanting to take lessons from Faraday on how to be a tough outlaw, for he turned his attention back to his boss, ignoring what was going on behind him. Geraldine got up and was moving toward the man's backside, pulling a stickpin out of the tiny hat she wore. For an old woman, she had guts, by God I'll give her that.

I saw Asa standing by the front door with something in his hand, although I couldn't make out what, and Wash was silently moving in from the far side of the room.

Faraday must have been so obsessed with his collection duties that he'd ignore anyone else who might be getting in the way. So it thoroughly surprised him when, as soon as he'd slapped Zeke Grant, Chance pulled a double-barreled shotgun off the rack and stuck it right in his face.

'I didn't like you when I saw you this morning,' Chance growled, 'and I like you even less now. Want to find out if this is loaded?' He was walking as he spoke, only two big strides taking him to where he wanted to be, with the end of the barrel sticking right into Faraday's face. Then, with one quick move, Chance executed a butt stroke that caught the man right under the chin, brought him standing to an upright position, then falling over backward, unconscious.

While Chance made his move, I was doing my own quick walk, although not as fast as my son. I needn't have worried, for Geraldine had the situation well in hand. By the time I reached her, both she and I knew exactly where she was going to plant that stickpin in her hands.

She stuck the man who'd knocked her down square in the ass.

'Mind your manners, sonny!' she yelled at the same time the man let out a terrifying scream.

I grabbed his arm and spun him around to face me, although he didn't seem to be concerned at that moment. When I grabbed him by the throat and began beating his face in, he got real concerned, but only for a second or two. I didn't know him from Adam. When he hit the floor, no one else would know that face either.

'Good for you!' Geraldine yelled, giving me a slap on the back.

While my opponent was falling down, I saw what it was that Asa had been holding in his hand. It was an iron skillet, and he'd used it on the third man, who'd tried to escape by the front door. From the look of that skillet and the man's face—both of which were bloodied considerably—I'd wager the two had met. The man was resting right beside the yahoo I'd felled.

I knew there was a fourth man, but didn't see him anywhere to my front or sides. Reflex had me pulling the Remington from my holster as I turned to my rear, but Wash had beaten me to it. Oh, the man was behind me all right. In fact, he was halfway through pulling out his own gun, and likely would have put a slug in my back. But like I said, Wash beat me to it.

'That'll be the worst mistake you make today, friend,' my son said as he pushed the barrel of his Dance Brothers pistol up against the man's temple. The man had to be a fool not to know that Wash was fixing to blow his brains out. He dropped the gun like it was a hot potato.

Geraldine silently handed me a rag and I wiped the blood off my fist, making my way to the last of these vermin who was conscious. He still had a scared look about him, and I was determined to keep it that way.

'Mister, I have an intense dislike for people who try to kill me,' I said with a growl and a hard, deep frown. I spit on his boot, daring him to do something about it, then said, 'You know, them Blackfeet up in the Shinin' Mountains got a real test to see how sandy a body is. Yes sir. Stake you to the ground and proceed to cut tiny slivers of your skin off enough to grab, then peel 'em back like a potato skin. Feisty lot, they are.' I had him sweating now, fearing for his own life. Once I saw that fear in the man, I knew he was going to do exactly what I wanted him to do, just to keep from getting the Blackfoot treatment.

'But you're in luck, amigo,' I continued in the same voice. 'Today you're gonna be a messenger for me.'

'Yes, sir,' he said, all of a sudden real accommodating to my wishes. 'Anything you say.'

'Good. Now, you seen what happened here.' I spread a hand over the limp bodies of his cohorts, who were still bleeding and still unconscious. His head moved up and down real fast. 'Well, these fellows are going to jail. But I've got designs for you that I think you're gonna like.'

'Anything you say, marshal. Anything you say.'

'You go see this Thad Wayne character. Tell him you want your wages and tell him what happened here. Then you find you your horse and ride like the wind. West, I'd advise. They's a couple of good fishing spots up in the Shinin' Mountains ary you look hard enough. I was you, I'd think real hard about finding another profession, cause this one ain't cut out for you, son. Or you ain't cut out for it, one. But you keep two things in mind all the while.'

'Yes, sir. What's that?' He was real humble by now.

'First off, don't ever say I didn't do nothing for you except give you a hard time, for you're getting a real break here.'

I paused, pulling my Remington out to check the loads. There was a purpose, for I don't usually do something like that in an idle manner.

'What's the other thing?' he asked impatiently, wanting in the worst way to get out of there.

'If I ever see you in Texas again, I'll shoot you on sight!' I spit it out like so much venom.

'Yes, sir! You won't ever see me again! Guaranteed!' he yelled, and broke and ran out of there as fast as he could. I knew he'd follow my orders.

Geraldine was tending to Zeke Grant, dabbing at the blood at the side of his mouth. He was shook up, mind you, but Zeke Grant was looking a whole lot more relieved than before Faraday and his bunch had waltzed into his store that night.

'What's going on here?' Marshal Dunston said as he walked in, gun in hand. When he looked at the bloodied bodies on the floor, he shook his head. 'I can't figure it out.'

'What's that?' Chance asked.

'You either can't stay away from trouble or you take this job seriously.'

'Can't stay away from trouble,' Chance said with a grin.

'Actually, we take the job seriously,' Wash added.

'It's a bit of both,' I said to clarify the matter. 'Sort of runs in the family. You get these birds over to jail and the four of us will write up statements for you on what happened here. These fellas are going to jail.'

Wash and Chance gave Ray Dunston a hand getting Faraday and his crowd over to the jail, while Asa took a seat and caught his breath.

Me, I had to talk to Miss Geraldine.

CHAPTER FOURTEEN

Davy Farnsworth told us it was just fine if we wanted to bed down in his livery overnight. Asa and me and my boys had gotten used to sleeping on the hard ground on this trek; fact of the matter is, we preferred it to beds some of these town hotels furnished a body with. I knew it had taken me a while to get used to a bed in Margaret Ferris's boardinghouse once I'd moved into the place. I reckon beds are as different as a decent pair of boots; you've got to get them broken in right to appreciate them properly. Like I say, I'd been married to Cora for a good thirty years and some, so it took a while to get used to her not being at my side, if you get my drift. Be that as it may, the four of us had been sleeping on a bed provided by Mother Nature for upwards

146

of a week now and had gotten used to it. Hell, growing up in this land, why, you never got unused to sleeping out of doors with the furnishings of Mother Nature about you. No sir. So a mite of straw was real comforting to us that night, thank you kindly.

'Doc Grizzard sure did have his hands full when we left the marshal's office,' Chance said as he rolled out his blanket that night.

'I expect,' I said, doing the same to my own blanket.

'I'll say,' Wash added with a laugh. 'Why, when he gets down to it, he can cuss up a storm near as good as you, Pa.'

'Are you bragging or complaining?' I asked.

'You best pass on that, if you're smart, son,' Asa said, although I thought I saw the hint of a smile on his lips as he spoke. It was instances like this that got me to wondering just how much Doc Grizzard knew about medicine, for if Asa was in constant pain, he sure didn't show it much. He'd seemed right ambitious to do away with Faraday earlier in the evening too. Either he enjoyed pain or ignored it. The only thing that really gave away the fact that he was injured was his shortness of breath at times, to a notable degree when he'd been walking a long distance or been more active than usual, like tonight.

'Say, what did you and that old woman

talk about while we were gone?' Chance asked. I knew he'd be the one to ask before the others would for the boy had a natural curiosity about him, which is likely why he managed to stay in so much trouble since he'd been able to walk and talk.

'Never you mind, son,' I replied in a stern manner. 'We had us a nice little talk about this and that. Suffice it to say I'm convinced that what Zeke Grant said about her is right. She'd rather walk through hell with a bucket of water and put out the fire her little own self before she'd help out Thad Wayne.'

Chance didn't do much more than let out a 'Harrumph' sound, which also seemed to satisfy the others. The sun was nearly down, and they were all about to pull their blankets over them when I suggested that we each take a turn at standing guard that night. At first they wanted to know whether I was out of my mind or not, but when I reminded them that we had done some serious damage to this Thad Wayne and his operation and that he was likely madder than the four of us all put together, they agreed. After all, even the marshal called it quits at night and left a night man to sit up with his prisoners. There was no reason we shouldn't take care to watch our own gear, especially our supplies. Especially, after I gave it second thought, Otis.

I took the first watch and was soon joined

by young Davy Farnsworth. I wasn't sure whether he was used to staying up later than we were or if he couldn't sleep and wanted someone to talk to, and I said as much to the boy.

'That's right smart, setting up a guard like that,' he said when he plunked himself down not far from where I was hunkering. I reckon he saw the Henry I had available just in case trouble started.

'How's that, son?'

He took a glance at the sky and said, 'Clear sky and a good enough moon to see with. It's the kind of night a body'd pull a raid of sorts. And if what I heard about what you fellas did tonight to Wayne's bunch of henchmen is right, why, I'd suspicion them trying something too.'

'Well now, son, you keep philosophizing like that, and folks hereabouts are gonna think you're a full-grown man,' I said with half a smile. I didn't want the boy to think I was joshing him, for manhood never is a thing to take lightly, whether you're as full grown a man as Jim Bridger or somewhere between hay and grass, like Kit Carson and me when we first started out with the mountain men. Damn, but that seemed like a long time ago.

'I ain't got no choice about it, Marshal Carston,' he said. I noticed he was looking the other way when he said it, as though not

149

wanting to see the emotion that was welling up inside him over the statement. I thought I heard him sniffle when he added, 'My folks are both gone now, and it's a hard land out here, so I ain't got no choice but to get tough and grown-up.'

'Do tell,' I said, hoping the boy would open up to me, for he surely did appear to have something eating away at his insides, and no man should have to feel that bad. He didn't disappoint me.

'It just doesn't seem fair that men like Thad Wayne should get away with the stuff they do when my pa and the others do all the work.' He slammed a fist into his hand and I saw how big his bony fist really was, realizing perhaps just how fast this lad was growing into a man.

'I know how you feel, son.' I said. 'That's why I took to wearing a badge. Seems to me there's just too many of them and not enough of us, but I never did give up trying to cut those odds down a mite.'

'Seems to me you did a good job of it tonight.'

'Well, thank you, son, I appreciate that,' I said, feeling a geniune warmth run through me and a good deal of respect for the boy-man who had spoken those words. All too often a man does nothing more than his job and hardly gets a pat on the back and a kick in the ass, usually at the same time, over what he's done. I'd learned a long time ago in the rangers that it's something special when you can get a decent compliment from the people whose land and property you are protecting, so Davy's comment was a welcome surprise to me.

The trouble was that with all that flattery, why, I wasn't quite sure where our conversation was leading or what else I could say to the boy. What I did know was that young Davy Farnsworth was at a delicate point in his life where, with no parents to guide him, he had only himself to rely on. And like Davy had said, this was a hard land. The strong were the ones who survived in it, and on more than one occasion a man will find it awful hard to pull all of his strong together to fight for something he believes in, especially when it's a lot easier to just move on and start all over, like a lot of folks in this land did. But then a man's got to live with himself too, and sometimes I reckon that takes more strength than facing the whole of the Comanche Nation all by your lonesome. Yes sir.

'You know, Davy, I was somewhere around ten or twelve when my mama died and I left home,' I said after a few minutes of silence between us. 'I disremember the exact age.' I was looking out into the night, piecing my story together and trying to keep a lookout at the same time. 'As I recollect, I

151

roamed about for a year or two before I signed up with Ashley and Henry on that first expedition they taken up the Arkansas. Met Kit Carson that year too.'

'You know Kit Carson!' the boy exclaimed excitedly. Most every boy I'd run into out here, including my own brood, had heard of and admired Kit Carson like he was some sort of giant in this land, and perhaps he was. If ever there was a man who could be classified as a genuine frontiersman, it was Kit.

'Better part of forty years, I'd say,' I said with a wink and a nod. 'Old Kit, he makes his home down in Taos now, I hear tell.'

'Boy, I'd sure like to meet him some day.' It was the boy in him coming out now, the part of a man that grows the most, for it seeks the same kind of pride and hero worship when it's five as when it's fifty. You can argue all you want, hoss, but as far as I'm concerned, admiration ain't nothing more than a grown-up version of hero worship. Yes sir.

'Play your cards right and you might some day,' I assured the lad.

'I'll bet he's tough.'

'Oh, he can be,' I said, 'but he don't make a habit of it all the time. I reckon that's the difference between him and these men like Faraday we had to deal with tonight.'

'What's that?'

152

'Well, Davy, it's men like Kit Carson who got their wits about 'em near all the time,' I said, wanting to place my words carefully. 'They know what's going on around them, and they know when they need to be tough and when compassion is called for. More importantly, they know the difference between the two.

'Yahoos like Faraday and his lot, why, they ain't worried about nothing more than impressing you with how tough they are. And if there's one thing I've learned, son, it's that if a man has to worry as constantly about how he's looked upon by other men, why, he sure isn't much of a man.'

'Yeah,' Davy said, nodding his head in agreement, 'I see what you mean. I reckon it's more important that you be yourself, huh?'

'I'll bet your pa told you that,' I said with a smile.

'Yeah,' he replied with a sheepish grin.

'One of the most misunderstood things about being a child is that you've got to hear from someone else what it is your mama and daddy tell you.'

'Yeah, I guess it is.'

'Davy, you just remember all those things your mama and daddy told you, and remember that they're more than likely true, and you'll grow up straight as one of them redwoods I seen so many years back. Just don't be in such an all-fired hurry to be tough and mean, or you'll wind up like Thad Wayne, and I know you got better in you than that, boy.'

I knew he must have been feeling a good deal of pride over the words I'd just spoken. I say that because I recalled saying those words, or something like them, to each of my boys, and they'd both turned out to be pretty good men.

It was about then that he rode up.

He looked big even riding in on his horse, except he wasn't riding. The bay he sat upon was a horse I'd gauge to have a lot of bottom, but it was obvious that he'd been ridden hard that day and the rider had the good sense to know when to let the animal walk at his own pace, as it did now.

'Got room for one more tonight?' he asked as he dismounted and Davy Farnsworth took the horse's reins. Davy had been right about the moon being out enough to see fairly well that night, for when he dismounted, I saw that he was armed to the teeth. He wore a wide-brimmed hat that hid his features pretty well until he took it off and slapped it against his trousers, sending dust flying all over the place. He'd been cradling a rifle in his left arm as he rode in, and maintained it there as he alit from his horse. He wore a buckskin jacket similar to my own, not an uncommon sight in this land, but it was what was beneath the jacket that caught my attention.

Although I couldn't tell for sure, I did know from the form of the butt of each of the revolvers stuck in his waistband that they were Colts, just like Chance's. I was sure that one was an Army Model .44 like Chance's, but thought the other might be a smaller model, perhaps a Colt Navy, which had been reissued in 1862 with only a few changes from its original 1851 model. I was sure that if this stranger were here long enough to meet Chance, the two would have a lot to talk about in the line of hardware.

He was somewhere around Chance's age, I reckon, although you can't really tell for sure in this land. But even in the moonlight I could see by the look in his eyes that this was a man who had aged, a man who had been places and done things, a man who was most likely in that damned war my boys were in. From that look and all that hardware, I had no doubt that he could be dangerous as well.

'Yes sir, I've got plenty of room in the livery,' Davy said. 'But I don't know if you'll be able to find a place to stay tonight. The only boardinghouse closes its doors to any new check-ins about eight or so, and it's past that.' At least Davy Farnsworth had learned the kind of manners from his parents that are needed to get along in this world, so he had that going for him, whether he knew it or

155

not.

A bit of a smile—a crooked one, I thought—appeared on the stranger's face. 'Well, I've been sleeping under the stars for the better part of a month now,' he said in an easy manner. 'Reckon one more ain't gonna hurt.'

'There's plenty of room in some of my empty stalls, if you like,' Davy volunteered. 'Just use the ones on the left. Most of the ones on the right are already taken.'

'Much obliged,' the stranger said with a nod. Then, untying his bedroll from his saddle, he added, 'Give the bay a good rubdown and the best of whatever feed you've got. This one deserves it.'

Davy told the man his daily rates, and the stranger dug down in a pants pocket and pulled out a coin tossing it to the boy. Then Davy got around to particulars.

'What'd you say your name was, sir?'

'I didn't.' There was nothing easy about the tone in his voice now, which had suddenly turned laconic. 'But if you're needing it for your records, it's Barnes.' He paused then, the way a man does who isn't sure of what he should say next, before adding, 'Jim Barnes.'

'Thank you, Mr Barnes,' Davy said, half apologetically, before taking the horse off to give him a good rubdown and feeding. I had half a notion the boy had asked who Jim

156

Barnes was more for my information than his own. The boy was proving to have his wits about him, just like Old Kit.

'Nice evening,' Barnes said to me in a conversational tone.

'That's a fact,' I said.

It had either been a long day or the two of us had already reached a point where the conversation was drying up real quick. Or maybe both. There was a bit of silence next, wherein the two of us just sized one another up in the moonlight.

'Hunting bear, are you?' he asked upon seeing the Henry I held in the crook of my own arm.

I shrugged noncommittally. 'Never can tell.'

I thought I saw that crooked smile come back to his face in the semidarkness.

'Had a run-in with one of them my own self,' he said with that smile. 'Wasn't as prepared as you are, though.'

Then, without waiting for an answer, he disappeared into the night.

I want you to know that even after I got off my shift at guard that night, I slept real light. Real light.

CHAPTER FIFTEEN

It was Asa who nudged me and brought me awake. It wasn't daylight yet, but I thought I saw a hint of orange beyond the door of the livery. Davy had pointed out where the well water was located, so I sloshed some in my eyes to wake up, and soon saw the stranger, Jim Barnes, beside me.

'Ain't nothing like cool water,' was all he said as he took my bowl and refilled it to do the same procedure I had.

'Ain't that the truth.'

The sun always seems to be a bit quicker rising than it does setting. I suppose one of those fellows who reads a lot and does a lot of deep thinking has got it all pegged as having to do with the length of the day that has the sun setting slower than it rises. But I never did pay much attention to those fellows, for most of them had never worked from 'can see to can't see' the way nearly everyone on the frontier does. Ain't nothing but pilgrims, if you ask me!

What the early-rising sun does do is allow a body to take in what's about him real quick, and I started doing that with Jim Barnes. He had soft blue eyes that seemed to be able to turn hard as slate in a second's notice, if you know what I mean. Like I say,

I'd determined the night before that he was a dangerous man, and part of that determination had come from the look in his eyes. This morning he seemed like a friendly enough sort. His hair was a mite on the longish side, finger-combed straight back and flowing down to his shoulders. At first glance it looked brown, although it might have been dirty blond if it had been freshly washed, which this man's hair wasn't. He didn't sport a beard, but he did have a mustache like Chance. He was a good six feet tall and maybe a couple of inches more, nearly as tall as me, I gauged. (It's funny about a man's vanity. Some have got the confidence to measure themselves back to back with a man in his stocking feet, while others are forever looking for some way to add a few more inches to their height, like adding their two-inch boot heels or that newfangled John B., a 'ten gallon hat' they were calling it.) This Jim Barnes seemed pretty well-proportioned, and looked as though he could handle himself in a tough spot. The only thing about him that I noticed was that he tended to favor his left arm when it came to lifting anything mighty heavy, which I took to be nothing more than the after-effects of a war wound.

'You been in this town enough to find a decent eatery, friend?' he asked after we'd stood there and took care of ourselves in

159

silence for more than a few minutes.

'Reed's Café up the street,' I said, tossing a thumb over my shoulder. 'If they tell you they got the best food in town, I suspicion it's likely because they're serving the only homemade food in town,' I added with a half smile, not wanting to give the man the impression that I was being a smart-aleck.

'Know what you mean,' he said, and gathered up an already dirty towel.

I pulled out my pocket watch and took a gander at it. It wouldn't be long before it was six o'clock and the Reed café would be opening. 'I'll be heading that way shortly, ary you care to join us,' I offered.

Jim Barnes shrugged, nodded. 'Sounds good. Ain't had no one to talk to but my horse and myself for the last month or so. Finding out what's going on in the rest of the world would be a real pleasure.'

I know I made a big deal of us Carstons hardly ever speaking once the food has been set before us, but you've got to realize that there is a good deal of palavering that goes on before and after the meals. Believe me, jawing can be just as much a part of the meal as putting away whatever it is that's warm and tasty on your plate, especially when what you're imparting is news of particular interest to the person you're talking to. Yes sir. News traveled awful slow in this part of the country. Unless, of course, it was some massacre by the Indians or something else. Like the fall of the Alamo. You know what I mean. Why I remember hearing about the fellow who stopped a lone wagon headed west and wouldn't let them proceed until they'd told him every morsel of news they'd heard from back East, the man was that starved for information about the world. Had them sitting there next to a fire for the better part of two days before he let them go, as I recall.

I got Wash and Chance up and introduced them to Jim Barnes, who they'd missed meeting the previous night when he rode in, and we were soon on our way to Reed's Café, Asa included. Davy Farnsworth said he wasn't much on breakfast and had to look after the horses, so we left him there alone. The more I was around Davy, the more I was getting the impression that he was a good solid boy who would turn into a fine young man one of these days. He seemed to have the right attitude and manners. What he needed to get over was the death of his father, and how long that would take was anybody's guess.

When we found a table long enough to seat all five of us, Carrie had coffee on the table in a jiffy, and was ready to take our orders in just as short a time. When she left to help her pa fix our orders, Jim Barnes, who was seated next to me, leaned over ever so slowly and pulled back my buckskin jacket, revealing the U.S. Deputy Marshal's badge pinned to my chest.

'Well, I'll be dammed,' he murmured in wonder.

'Something wrong with that?' Chance all but growled. The boy's not worth a damn in the mornings until he's had a cup or two of the hot black stuff, and he was only on his first cup now.

He smiled back at my son. 'Not a thing.' Then, slowly pulling back the left side of his own buckskin jacket, he said, 'I've got one of them my own self.' By the time he was through talking, he had pulled back the inside of the jacket far enough for all of us to see the same U.S. Deputy Marshal's badge that I was wearing, pinned on the inside of his jacket. As soon as he knew we'd all seen his badge, he dropped the jacket back in place. He sure didn't seem in any hurry for the word to get around that he wore the federal badge. No wonder he had a dangerous look about him, I found myself thinking.

'Well, I'll be damned,' Asa said, and I swear his jaw dropped half a foot. The way I figure it, Asa wasn't as surprised at the fact that the man next to him was a federal lawman as he was that he now had two federal lawmen in the same town. I knew that getting his boys out of jail was still heavy on his mind. I was just hoping he didn't figure I'd forgotten them, for I hadn't.

'That's what I said,' Jim Barnes replied.

'I assume you're not here on some kind of pleasure trip, then, marshal,' Wash said in as pleasant a manner as he could, something not easy for him, whether early in the morning or late at night. Like I said, the boy's got a whole different disposition than his brother.

'You'd figure right,' Jim Barnes said.

Carrie brought out a huge tray full of steaming plates, and took her time setting them down before us, making sure everyone got the right order. We were all silent while she did her business, except for Jim, who took the chance to tell her she served right fine-tasting coffee. That got him a bit more attention as she set his plates down, along with a big smile of gratitude to go along with it. From the look in her eyes, I had a distinct notion that she was ready for him to court her or her to start tucking his shirttail in. I also had a notion that would be hard to do with this Jim Barnes, for he was a man who drifted a lot, of that I was certain. It was after she left and we'd dug into the meal that we went back to occasionally talking about our business, namely the law.

'I ain't too anxious to let it be known I'm the law,' Jim said after five minutes and half of his plate of eggs had disappeared. 'Been

163

looking for some army deserters and horse thieves, so I've got to play my cards close to my vest.'

'I know what you mean,' I said briefly, once I felt my mouth was sufficiently empty enough to get a word or two in. I also went on, in just as brief a manner, to explain to Jim Barnes the why and wherefore of how we came to be in this place called Hogtown.

'Still in jail, are they?' Jim asked Asa.

Before Asa could answer, I said, 'We're planning to rectify that situation today, as a matter of fact.' I winked at Asa. 'Yes sir.'

Our plates were clean, just the way Mama always told us to clean them, and we were all on a third or fourth cup of coffee, when Wash pushed himself away from the table and sloshed on his hat.

'If you'll excuse me, I do believe I'll head on down to the livery and see about packing some of those goods we bought yesterday,' he said, to my surprise. Then he let slip his real motive for leaving. 'Besides, maybe I can give young Davy a hand with some of the chores. That livery is a fair-sized operation from what I've seen.'

'Think I'll go along with you,' Asa said, also getting up from the table.

'Listen, Asa, I don't want you doing any work down there,' I said in a serious manner. 'You know what Doc Grizzard said.'

The man looked taken aback. 'Work? I

164

ain't gonna do no work! Hell, somebody's gonna have to supervise these young'uns.' Then his look of mock surprise turned into a smile as he planted his own hat atop his head and left with Wash. If he was hurting, at least he still had a sense of humor about him.

Jim Barnes and I sat and talked over coffee, while Chance ordered another handful of eggs to go along with the remaining biscuit or two on the table. After listening to Barnes talk about how he'd been chasing these horse thieves and army deserters for upwards of two months as a U.S. Deputy Marshal, I had little doubt about the far-reaching authority the badge and the man holding the position held. Like I said, I'd yet to give the federal law books a thorough reading, but if a man like Jim Barnes could head down to Texas to go after horse thieves and deserters who were originally wanted in Missouri, why, I shouldn't have to worry about my own presence in Hogtown. No sir.

It was maybe a half hour later when I heard the door open behind me and turned to see a distressed looking Geraldine enter the café and make her way toward our table. I pulled out my pocket watch and saw that it was past seven o'clock but not yet eight, when a good many of the merchants opened for the day's business. It seemed kind of strange for this old woman to be up about this early in the morning. Of course, I wasn't exactly thrilled to see her looking as exasperated as she was either.

'Well now, darlin', ain't it kind of early for a woman of your stature to be out in this town?' I said, trying to be calm about the whole thing.

'You know good and well it's Miss Geraldine's big ears that's got her here this early, Pa,' Chance said, the smart-aleck coming out in him even when he dealt with his elders.

'My eye and Betty Martin!' the old woman shot back at Chance with a sharp look, matched only by her voice. 'It ain't my ears that's big, sonny, it's that *big mouth* of Thad Wayne!'

'Well now, if that don't—'

'Shut up, Chance,' I said without looking at him. Once Geraldine had mentioned Thad Wayne, I had an urgent notion that the news wasn't going to be all that good, and Chance's sense of humor meant little or nothing to me. I noticed that young Jim Barnes had taken an interest in the old woman now too.

'What is it, Miss Geraldine?' I asked once she had taken a seat and gotten her breath back.

'Bad news, marshal,' she said, still gasping a little, although speaking as clearly as I'd ever heard her speak in the short time I'd known her.

'You mentioned Thad Wayne.'

'Yes. I was wandering around his place early this morning, looking for firewood,' she said by way of explanation. 'It's amazing what you can find for firewood in the back of these places. Purely amazing.'

'Go on,' I urged. She had me both excited and worried at the same time.

'Why, I came upon Thad Wayne himself, I did. He was out back shaving and giving orders to one of his henchmen, I reckon. And what I heard, why it's just awful, marshal, awful!'

'And what's that, Geraldine!'

'I tell you, that Thad Wayne is a mean one, yes sir. Why, do you know he's gonna burn one of the buildings at the edge of town? Figures on teaching the town a lesson, he does.'

'He said that, did he?' Chance asked, any humor now gone from his tone. I had a notion he was thinking along the same lines as me.

'You betcha, sonny,' she said with a wink and a nod. 'Trouble is, he didn't say which building he was gonna burn at the edge of town.'

'I think I know what he's talking about,' Chance said, wiping his face with his napkin. He was clearly through eating for the morning. Next, he pulled out his Colts and

167

silently began checking the loads, an action that startled Geraldine.

'What's that?' Jim Barnes asked, speaking up for the first time since the old woman had entered the café.

'We just came from it, Jim,' I said. 'I'd bet a dollar it's Davy Farnsworth's livery they're planning on hitting.' I turned my attention back to Geraldine. 'When did Wayne say he was gonna do this firing up?'

'That's what I been trying to tell you!' she all but screamed at me. 'Now! After breakfast!'

It was all I needed to hear as my own fears set me in motion. I didn't bother checking my loads on the Remington as I pushed back my chair, rose and planted my hat on my head, all in one motion, I didn't even invite anyone else to come along as I strode toward the door and made my way toward the livery. I knew that Chance wouldn't be far behind me. I could count on that. As for Jim Barnes, he could come or he needn't, the choice was his. Besides, I didn't know the man that well and had no right to ask him to take part in my own troubles. This was turning into a family affair, and us Carstons pretty much take care of ourselves when it comes to that.

From what I'd seen so far, I could stand up to any one of this bunch of amateurs that Thad Wayne employed, for none of them had impressed me at all. Hell, I was prepared to stand up to them all by myself if that was what it called for. It wouldn't be the first time I'd done something foolish like that. It was what I was aware of that was bothering me. It had become pretty evident that Wayne's men liked to work in bunches, like wolves, so he'd likely send a handful of men to do the job of firing up young Davy Farnsworth's livery. What I also knew for a fact was that Wash and Asa had taken off back to the livery not long ago, and would be there when Wayne's men made their move on the livery.

'What's your hurry, Pa?' Chance asked as he caught up with me halfway there. 'You ain't worried about Wash, are you? Hell, he'll save a few of the bastards for us. He's a good man, you know.' The words almost made me fall over in shock as I stopped dead in my tracks. I couldn't recall either one of the boys pay any kind of compliment to the other in their lifetime, so Chance's words expressing confidence in his brother about threw me for a loop.

'Actually, son, I'm worried about Asa,' was my reply in a straight face. 'He might decide to take on the whole gang, and get himself killed in the process.' I continued walking at a good pace then, not giving my son a chance to make any more smart-alecky remarks. Besides, I wasn't about to tell him that I was more worried about Davy

Farnsworth than I was about my boy or Asa.

When I stopped to make comment on Chance's remark, I'd also taken quick notice that neither Jim Barnes nor anyone else seemed to be following us toward the trouble I knew was waiting for us at the livery.

Thad Wayne's men had already struck the livery when Chance and I arrived. Three yahoos were fighting Davy, Asa, and Wash one on one, with Wash being the only one who seemed to be holding his ground. I could tell by the grimace on his face that Asa was feeling ten times the amount of pain the man hitting him was dishing out. As for Davy Farnsworth, the boy could hit his mark real well, he just didn't have any bulk to hold him down, for whenever his opponent hit him he went flying back a half-dozen feet, most times landing on his keister.

It was the fourth man, standing off to the side, who bothered me the most. He held a lit torch in his hand and seemed to be taking the whole melee in, as though he were some spectator. Geraldine had been right, they were here to torch the livery! I pulled my Remington out and shot the torch out of his hand. He grabbed his wrist, dropping the torch on some loose hay at his feet.

'Put that goddamn fire out,' I said as though he were some reckless schoolboy who had made a terrible mistake and was about to answer to his teacher.

I knew the situation was well in hand when I heard Chance pull his own Colt out, cock it and say, 'You heard him, mister. I'd get that bucket of water unless you want to die wondering why you're acting so ignorant.'

Me, I walked behind the big brute who was beating the hell out of Asa and sunk a hard right fist into his side. Like I said, all you have to know is that they don't play by any rules. So fair fight be damned. Asa was getting up off the ground, an agonizing look of pain on his face as he put all of his energy into getting back on his two feet. I knew then that no one would ever accuse Asa Wilson of being short on guts. I spun this bully around to face me and commenced to beat on his head, neck and shoulders with all my might. He was bleeding and unconscious when he fell to the ground in a lifeless hulk.

Wash had some blood dribbling down his chin, but he was holding his own far better than young Davy, who at the moment seemed to be closing in on death, his opponent holding him fast in a bear hug.

'Bite the son of a bitch!' Chance yelled out behind me, and Davy did just that.

Like a rattler looking for the right place to strike, Davy turned his head sideways and leanded over far enough to bite the man's ear, and he did it good and hard. The man let out a horrendous scream of pain, and let go of Davy. The boy was fast thinking on his feet, and gave the man two good fistfuls in the face once he'd gotten his balance.

That's when Chance stepped in. He grabbed the man, who was about to go after Davy again, spun him around and hit him twice in the gut, placed two huge hands around his head and brought his knee up and the man's head down at the same time. Chance had a mite of blood on his pants leg, and the man had a good deal of blood all over his face when he hit the ground. A broken nose will do that for you.

'You know where all the right places to hit are, son,' Chance said to Davy, 'but you're practicing too much on being fair about how you fight.'

'I'm afraid I'm not your size yet, Mr Carston,' the boy said, out of breath.

'Well, I'll tell you what, son,' Chance said, placing a friendly hand on the boy's shoulder, 'whenever you've got to fight some coyote like this one, you kick him in his elsewheres and you'll have all the time you want in the world to hunt up a good strong piece of wood and knock his brains out.'

Wash was getting the better of the man he was fighting when I heard another gun cock off to the side. When I turned I saw it was the torch holder, the one Chance had made put the fire out. I was about to ask Chance how he could let this man get by him like he had, but the man was speaking now.

'You just hold it right there, all of you,' he said in what I took to be a rather shaky voice. 'Mr Wayne wanted a job done, and it's gonna get done.'

'Words like that get a man in trouble.' The words sounded awful familiar, although I wasn't sure I could place them. It was when Jim Barnes stepped out into the open from the same boardwalk Chance and I had come down, that I recognized them. Hell, he hadn't done all that much talking, so how was I to know it was him? 'Now, you put that gun down and keep your mouth shut before you get into all sorts of trouble.'

'And who the hell are you?'

'You don't really want to know, do you, Wallace? I found them horses you stole just outside of town last night, before I arrived here. I figured you weren't far behind.' Apparently, this was one of the horse thieves Jim Barnes was after. It was then I noticed that Barnes didn't appear to have a gun in his hands, had his hands down by his sides, in fact. A crooked sort of smile came to his face as he peeled back the inside of his buckskin jacket and watched a good deal of fear culminate in the eyes of the man he was addressing. Mind you, the other man was the one holding the gun, yet Barnes smiled as though he had him cold.

And maybe he did.

In one quick move Wallace, or whoever he

173

was, swung his point of aim from me to Jim Barnes. It was the wrong move. It was also the last move that Wallace made in his life, for quick as you please, Jim Barnes had a gun in his hand—hidden by his right side, I thought—and put a slug in Wallace's heart. The man was dead before he hit the ground, his shot fired wild.

'That's one I come after,' Barnes said as he put his Colt back in his waistband.

'I do believe we've got a few more of Wayne's crowd for you to feed, marshal,' I said, a hint of a smile on my lips. But my words were wasted on the city marshal, for he turned his attention to Jim Barnes, who we were all discovering was a deadly man indeed.

'I hope you don't plan on staying around here much longer, mister,' Ray Dunston said impatiently as he took in the scene before him. When Jim Barnes said nothing, only pulling back his buckskin jacket to show his U.S. Deputy Marshal's badge to the city marshal, it didn't seem to impress Ray Dunston at all. No sir. 'I don't give a damn what kind of tin you're wearing mister,' he added, a growl in his voice now. 'Believe me, I know a killer when I see one.'

I looked at the body of Wallace, then back at Jim Barnes, who stood there as cool as a cucumber. I knew what Dunston was getting at, for I figured I knew a killer when I saw one too.

And I was looking at one right now.

CHAPTER SIXTEEN

Of the five of us who had taken part in fighting off Thad Wayne's crowd, it was Wash and Davy Farnsworth who seemed to have the most blood about them from the fracas. But I was willing to bet a dollar that it was Asa Wilson who'd suffered the most, especially when you consider how much damage was likely done to the man's insides more than his outsides. I had no doubt that Wash and Davy, being the youngest of the lot, would have no trouble recovering. The young ones seldom did. And if I sound like I'm leaving out Jim Barnes, well, maybe it's because he dealt a hand in the whole mess after it was mostly over. Even if he did save our lives.

Wash threw a handful of water on his face, swished some around in his mouth to get rid of the blood he swallowed, and volunteered to stay at the livery to keep an eye on things while Davy helped Asa Wilson over to Doc Grizzard's office.

'I don't need no attention, Will, honest,' Asa had pleaded with me, but I reminded him that the good doctor had wanted him to stop by again today anyway to get another dose of that salve he was putting on his wound and to retape his ribs. It gave Asa a legitimate excuse for going to see Doc Grizzard. I didn't say it, but it gave me a pure feeling of relief to be able to get the man to the doctor's office too. I've seen men who got busted up inside, and it ain't a pretty sight once they get all bandaged up and told by some sawbones that they had to stay in bed or risk the chance of dying from their wounds.

Davy was acting like he might have a stove-in rib or two also, although the more obvious thing to take care of on the boy was his bloodied-up face. I could tell he'd taken some pretty tough blows from that yahoo who had set himself on the young livery owner, for he was bleeding from the mouth some and had the makings of a black eye about him. I'd recalled experiencing all of it in my youth, and let me tell you, there ain't none of it designed to make a body look any more pleasing to the girls in the village. No sir.

'Make sure and take your time getting over to Doc's office, fellas,' Chance said.

'Why's that, son?' Asa asked.

Chance smiled as he said, 'Any two men who've fought on the same side oughtta have a chance to get their stories straight. Gives 'em both a chance to look like heroes when they got to explain to a doctor how busted up they come to be.'

'The only thing I want to get is taken care of so I can get back here and relieve Wash,' Davy said. 'He looks like he could use a mite of caring for too.' Once again I felt a stir of pride go through my body for Davy Farnsworth. The boy was showing signs of compassion, and I was glad, for it wasn't often you'd find a body interested in caring for a stranger. But then when you stand back to back with a man and dish out as good as you can in a fight, well, I reckon you get to be more than just strangers, whether you know one another on a first-name basis or not.

'That hero talk wasn't made for nothing but them dime novels I hear about,' Asa said.

'You done real fine, Asa,' I said as the two began to cross the street, heading for Doc Grizzard. 'I'll tell your boys what you done.'

'Obliged,' he said without turning his head back to face me. I reckon he figured we knew one another well enough to know that our word meant damn near everything to each of us. And it did.

We sloshed some water on the three hardcases laying on the livery grounds, none of us caring whether they came to in a mess of mud or not. In the meantime, Ray Dunston gave Jim Barnes a hand with

Wallace, wrapping the body up in a blanket and fixing to cart him off. So far Jim Barnes had impressed me as being the type of man who was more than a mite thorough in getting his job done. More than likely, he would be wanting Doc Grizzard to pronouce the man legally dead and write up a coroner's report for him to make things legal once he got back to wherever it was in Missouri he came from.

It took a bit of time to get Wayne's yahoos to the jail, for although they had been revived, they still didn't seem to have their wits about them. At least they didn't give us any trouble on the way to jail, staggering about like Saturday-night drunks after closing hours.

At the marshal's office the three were placed in a separate cell and told they would have to wait for Doc Grizzard to make his daily rounds before they'd be looked at. The only one who didn't seem somewhat relieved was Ray Dunston, who still had a harsh eye on Jim Barnes.

'I'll give you all the right forms to fill out, Barnes,' he growled once his prisoners were locked up, 'but you'll have to fill 'em out yourself.'

'I can read and write,' was Barnes's rather curt reply as he took the forms.

I noticed that all the while Dunston and Barnes had been taking one another in,

Chance had been standing next to the front door to the office, doing the same to both men, as though waiting to see which one would get froggy and leap. A frown now came to his face, the kind of frown that is more of a puzzle than done in anger. Something was bothering Chance about these two men, and I had a notion I'd find out what it was real quick. When Barnes grabbed the papers from Dunston and turned to leave, I found out exactly what was on my oldest boy's mind. Chance took a huge step to the side, blocking the door.

Jim Barnes frowned now himself, not sure what to make of the whole situation.

'I need to leave,' he said simply. 'Got work to do.' But Chance didn't seem concerned about that now.

'Seems to me I knew a fella like you once,' he said flat out. 'During the war, it was. I only seen him once.' Chance gave me a glance. 'Been bothering me ever since I seen him, Pa.' he added, before turning his attention back to Jim Barnes. 'About your size, I'd say.'

'As I recall, it was a long war with a lot of people in it,' Jim Barnes said by way of an explanation. 'I ain't the only one who stands a good six foot in his stocking feet.' A crooked grin came to his face now. 'Seems to me all three of you Carstons top that at least.'

179

'Only seen him from a distance,' Chance went on, ignoring anything the man before him might have said. 'But I'd swear he was wearing the same kind of flop hat you've got.'

Jim Barnes shrugged. 'I'm not the only one who wears this kind of cover.'

'Ary what I heard was right, he had the same last name's you,' Chance said, the frown in his forehead deepening as he spoke. The more information he gave forth, the more troubled he seemed to be over this relative stranger.

'Could've been distant relatives,' was the only explanation the federal lawman gave. He seemed as cool now as he had been under fire.

'Bill Barnes, that's what the name was.' Chance had dug back in his memory and remembered what it was he was searching for. Suddenly, I thought I saw a bit of worry come to Jim Barnes's face, as though Chance had gotten too close to something in his past, something that could really bother him. 'Shady character, he was. Some kind of shady work he did too.' Chance paused a moment, then I saw it in his eyes like about the same time that Jim Barnes did. Chance knew. Whatever it was he'd been searching for in the past, he'd found. And it concerned this Jim Barnes, this man Ray Dunston had called a killer.

'That war really made an impression on you, didn't it, Chance?' Barnes said, the crooked smile reappearing. The man had obviously made a decision and was in full control again.

'Had that effect on a lot of people, from what I understand.'

'Marshal,' Barnes said, addressing Ray Dunston now. 'Have you got any more cups?'

'Sure. Why?'

'Well,' he said, pushing his hat back and scratching his head, 'Chance here has put me between a rock and a hard spot. If you want to fill those cups up, I'll fill you all in on what it is Chance thinks he remembers. The only thing you've got to promise me is that all stays right here until I say different.'

Ray Dunston turned out to be as curious about the man as Chance and I were. Pulling out extra cups and filling them with coffee was the fastest I'd seen the city marshal move since I'd come to Hogtown. Yes sir, he was surely interested in this man.

Chance had been right about a lot of things. Bill Barnes was the name the man had used during the War Between the States. And it had been Jim Barnes who had been known back then as Bill Barnes. The reason the man had stayed pretty distant with most of the troops he come into contact with was because he had been a Union spy. From as many exploits as he'd had behind Confederate lines during the war, I wouldn't be surprised if Wash was the one would be saying that he had seen this Jim Barnes character too.

When Chance asked him about the change in his name, he explained—as he had to me earlier in the day at the livery—that he was after horse thieves and army deserters and didn't care to let everyone know what his real name was.

That was when he told us his real name.

I didn't know the name from Adam, but said I'd hold it in confidence until he said otherwise. Like I said, this was a land where a lot of young men were deciding to take up the trade of professional gunman.

Jim Barnes, he was just another up and comer to me.

CHAPTER SEVENTEEN

'That's Pa, all right,' Tom Wilson said with a chuckle. After Jim Barnes got through with his story, I'd been ready to go over to Doc Grizzard's to see how Davy Farnsworth and Asa were faring when I remembered that I'd told Asa I'd mention his deeds to his sons. I'd become so taken with the story young Barnes had told that I'd nearly forgotten about Jeremiah and Thomas Wilson. Somehow, they seemed to have gotten lost in the mess my boys and I had become embroiled in. Not that it should matter, for everything seemed to track right back to Thad Wayne in this town. Hell, everything began and ended with the man, or so it would seem. Still, it was good to see that the Wilson boys had maintained a sense of humor, especially after a couple of weeks in the Hogtown hoosegow.

The Wilson boys were just a tad taller than medium height, which placed them about a head shorter than my own boys, the same as Asa was about a head shorter than me. They had dark Indian eyes and brown hair and were as honest as I gauged my own boys to be. When I looked at the pair of them and compared them to my own sons, I had no doubt that Asa and I had done a better than average job of raising these lads.

'Yeah,' Jeremiah said with a smile, 'Pa'd charge Hell with a bucket of water, put out the fire, and skate on the ice.'

'Ain't that the truth,' I said, returning their smiles. On a more sober note, I added, 'I would have gotten here sooner, but there's been a whole lot going on around this town, and they sort of volunteered me to help 'em clean the mess up.'

'Wouldn't expect nothing less, Mr Carston,' Tom said. 'Pa always said you was the best lawman Twin Rifles ever had.'

'But what's this?' his brother asked in admiration, taking in my new lawman's badge. 'You've got new responsibilities, have you?'

'Hell, a man's got to be good at something,' Chance said as he approached the cell.

'Looks like you've grown a mite, Chance,' Tom said.

Chance smiled. 'I reckon we all have, Tom.'

'Say, what got you boys in this predicament, anyway?' I asked. 'I never did figure you for getting behind bars like this.'

'Neither did Pa,' Jeremiah said.

'So I hear.' I knew he was referring to Asa's attempt to get his boys freed a few weeks back, and the less than successful outcome.

'I reckon we happened to be the unlucky ones who were out on the boardwalk when the teller in the town bank got killed,' Tom said. I could see a good deal of anger well up in him as he recalled the event. Tom then lowered his voice and added, 'That marshal out there didn't want to listen to anything we had to say so I figured him for being one of this Thad Wayne's bunch. Figured I'd wait until the trial before I let on to what I know.'

'What's that, son?' I asked, feeling a certain amount of excitement over the boy's secret. That I recalled, Tom Wilson had always had a good memory.

All of a sudden, Jeremiah was as enthralled with his brother's mysterious knowledge as Chance and I were. 'You never said anything about that before,' he said now, speaking in a tone of voice as low as his brother's.

'Mind you now, these bank robbers had masks on, but I think I could recognize one or two of them,' Tom said.

At last I had something to go on, something that sounded like hard evidence! Maybe there was a way of getting this Wayne character put behind bars after all.

'Well, who—'

'You ain't gonna believe this, Mr Carston, but one of 'em's already in the hoosegow,' Tom interrupted with a grin. It was the kind of look a man has when he knows something you don't and is about to spring it on you right quick.

'And who might that be?' Chance said. We were all talking in hushed tones now.

'The one across the way,' Tom said, nodding toward a cell with three of Thad Wayne's men in it. 'The ugly one with the busted jaw. Black hair, bushy eyebrows.'

Faraday! By God, it was him all right. When I looked at Chance, I saw him smile at me, knowing he had picked out the same one I did.

'That makes you an eye witness.' I said.

'Then how about getting us out of this hole?' Jeremiah said. 'I don't think I can take much more of this kind of hospitality, not to mention the food.'

I found myself doing some quick thinking, trying to gauge what was going to happen next, what I could do next to trap Wayne and his men. At first, I'd had the same suspicion that the Wilson boys did about Ray Dunston, wondering whether he was one of Wayne's men who simply wore a badge and jumped whenever the man told him to. I was still tempted to believe that, for the man hadn't really done anything to help us along with our job. Oh, he'd been here in his office and tended to the prisoners, but he'd also supposedly been conveniently away from his office when Faraday and his crowd had escaped yesterday afternoon, in time to make their rounds of the local merchants to collect their extortion money. Then, out of the corner of my eye, I noticed that Jim Barnes was having a good talk with Ray Dunston, doing a real good job of keeping his attention. It was then it came to me.

'I'll tell you what, boys,' I said, still talking in low tones, 'I've got no doubt in my mind that you're innocent. And eventually you're gonna get out of this place. But for today I want you to stand pat.' I then gave them a bit of instruction on what I wanted them to do. 'Did I ever show you how well this jacket of mine's made, Tom?'

'No sir.'

'Well, you take a look at this,' I said, and pulled open the left side of my coat to reveal to him the stitching Cora had done on it so many years ago. Chance caught on real quick and made a similar statement to Jeremiah, who stood directly across from him.

The Wilson boys took their time admiring Cora's handiwork, although I have to tell you, they didn't know one hell of a lot about sewing. Let me just put it this way. When we left the marshal's office, Tom and Jeremiah felt real secure.

Real secure.

★   ★   ★

'They're doing just fine,' I said to Asa in Doc Grizzard's office. 'Look like they could use a good meal, but none the worse for wear, by my guess.'

Asa let out a sigh of relief. 'That really makes me feel better, Will. It really does.'

'Good.'

Doc Grizzard had put more salve on his wound and was just finishing up taping his ribs again. Davy Farnsworth had apparently already been taken care of, for it was Wash who was seated and waiting to be looked at next. Asa Wilson looked to be breathing a mite easier. Of course, I was surprised that he was still breathing at all after that run-in at the livery earlier this morning.

'Now, Mr Wilson, I'm not gonna tell you this again,' Doc Grizzard said, a stern look about him as he put away the tape. 'You'd better get some rest, a lot of it. If you don't I'm not going to be responsible for one of those ribs breaking and puncturing your lung. I mean it,' he added, shaking a finger at the man as though he were some schoolboy in for a scolding.

'Better do what the man says,' Chance said. 'I don't mind telling you that I don't favor having to drag your carcass back down this dusty trail, once this thing is all over. Getting you this far was hard enough.'

'He's right,' I said. 'Your boys have told me enough to make me think I could actually put this Thad Wayne character away.'

Doc Grizzard gave Wash a thorough looking over while Asa sat there and listened to Chance and me tell him what I'd found out from his boys. He took in every word as though he'd never heard it before, rather than being what he'd expected all along. The relief he felt about his boy's safety was more visible than any pain he might be feeling.

'The next time you bring this bunch in to be looked at, marshal, I'll likely ask you for some more money,' Doc said in a half serious tone. 'Your credit's about run its course in this office.'

'Believe me, Doc, I didn't set out to put these yahoos between a rock and a hard spot,' was my reply.

'Sure, sure.' You could tell he absolutely believed every word I'd said.

'What've you got in mind now, Pa?' Wash asked. I knew that if Chance had his way, he'd be heading for a saloon for a morning beer. Me, I had different designs.

'Well, son, it seems to me there's been an awful lot of talk about this Thad Wayne fella,' I said. 'I was thinking I'd find out where he hangs his hat and pay him a visit.'

* * *

Doc pointed out Thad Wayne's place, which wasn't far from his office. It was two blocks at most, all of which seemed to be an easy walk, although I wasn't sure whether Asa would make it in as quick a pace as us Carstons. As we left Doc Grizzard's place, he seemed to be walking a lot more cautious, as though the good doctor's words had finally sunk in. Or maybe it was the fact that he now knew for sure that his two boys were going to make it out of Hogtown, which after all was the primary reason for our visit in the first place.

'Are you sure you don't want to stay here with Doc?' I asked as we reached the bottom of the stairs outside the physician's office.

189

'Maybe lay down some, like Doc prescribed?'

Such a suggestion was all Asa Wilson needed to get his back up like any porcupine. 'Not hardly!' he said with a good deep voice. 'I want to see the son of a bitch who put my boys in jail, by God!' The man was clearly on fire about this particular subject and wasn't about to have it any other way.

'Don't blame you one bit, Asa,' Chance said in agreement. 'Just do me a favor, if you will.'

'What's that?'

'Don't shoot the bastard right off. I'd at least like to hear what he has to say for himself.'

'I got a feeling that ain't gonna be an awful lot, Chance,' Wash added.

'Let's just make sure we keep it all legal, boys,' I said, tossing in my own two cents' worth and hoping they took heed of what I was saying.

I should have known Thad Wayne's house from the moment I'd seen it. I recalled noticing it when we'd first ridden into town, although I gave it short shrift at the time. It was half again the size of a normal house you'd find in the city. But then that's the kind of luxury the Thad Waynes of this world figure they need to keep up their image. It's got to be bigger and better than anyone else's, if for no other reason than to

190

show that they can afford to have it done. The only thing that made it look anywhere close to the other houses in the town was the fact that it was painted white.

I made my way up the porch to the front door, Chance, Asa, and Wash in tow behind me. The man who answered the door had to be Thad Wayne, although I have to confess I was looking for some fancy kind of valet to do the door opening. Hired help was another way a man with money tended to do his bragging in a silent fashion, if you know what I mean. He was big and broad-shouldered, somewhere about the size of me or Chance.

'Come in, marshal,' he said in a deep resonant voice that bordered on the formal, or maybe educated is the word I'm looking for. 'I've been expecting you.'

'You're either good at second-guessing or you've been reading my mind, mister,' I said in reply. When he didn't say a hell of a lot in return, I had a notion that his formal airs were nothing but a front. It's been my experience that these back East-educated folks tend to rattle easy, as though in all that educating, no one ever taught them to talk back. A quirky breed they are.

'Please have a seat,' he said as he led us into his living room, which turned out to be a spacious area with a collection of fine furniture. I was tempted to take a seat when I noticed he remained standing.

191

He's a hideout-gun man, was the first thing that crossed my mind.

'No thanks,' I said, pushing my hat back on my head. 'Might cramp my style, especially ary a couple of your boys come busting through the kitchen back there.'

'Same with me,' Chance said, loosening the Colts in his holsters. 'I never did fancy dying in a seated position.'

'You're Thad Wayne, ain't you?' Asa said in a voice dripping with hatred. No beating around the bush for Asa Wilson, no sir.

'Yes, I am, old man,' Wayne said. 'Is there a reason you need to know that?'

'Just wanted to see what the man I'm gonna kill looks like,' Asa snarled. If he was in any kind of pain, he sure wasn't showing it, or didn't care about it, one. Fact of the matter was, I knew good and well that Asa could of killed the man where he stood. He likely would have too, if I hadn't placed a firm hand on his arm when I did.

'You'll have to forgive my friend here,' I said apologetically, 'but you put his two boys in jail for a crime they didn't commit, and he's come to get 'em out.'

Thad Wayne chuckled to himself. 'That's a bit impossible, my good man,' he said, fading back into that formal way of talking. 'They're being charged with murder, and if I do say so myself, that takes at least a good lawyer and a good many reliable witnesses to get out of.'

'Not necessarily, friend,' I said in an even voice. Thad Wayne was the kind of man. who made you want to brag like hell to him, just to get him to do something against you, but I knew that he'd likely run if you jumped in his direction. No sir, I was wanting to pull this man into a trap, one where he couldn't get away, couldn't run. This visit wasn't meant to do anything more than set the bait in place. And, as Asa said, to get a look at the man I was going up against.

'Oh,' Wayne said, raising an eyebrow to my words. It was easy to see that I was starting to bother him, which is just what I had in mind.

'Well, you see, friend, we got us an eye witness,' I said with half a smile, just to let him know I knew how he was feeling about all of this. 'One of Asa's boys, in fact.'

'Is that right.' He didn't seem to have the confidence he first had when we'd entered his house.

'Seen that whole botched job that Faraday and his boys did of robbing the bank here. Of course, we got Faraday in jail already, so we only got one man to hunt up.' I paused, waited in silence while the impact of what I'd said soaked into the man.

'And?'

'Once I find him, I'm sure he'll be willing to talk, especially if he's trading his neck for yours,' I said with a smile, which was a hell of a lot more confident than the look on his face.

'Are you threatening me?' The formality and education in his voice were gone now, replaced by the down-to-earth hardcase I knew Thad Wayne to be once you got past the front he put on.

'Pa threaten you?' Wash said in mock surprise. 'Why shoot, mister, Pa's a gentle man, he wouldn't threaten you.' My youngest tossed a thumb at his brother. 'Chance, now, he'd do something threatening. Asa too. Why, I might take a hand in some of that, ary it was a bad day. But not Pa.'

'And just what is it that you're passing on to me, if not a threat?' There was a good deal of anger in the man's tone.

'Using your own men to rob the town's bank wasn't too awful bright, Wayne,' I said. 'But then you greedy fellas usually ain't too bright. Town finds out you done this, and they'll run you out for sure.

'As for what I'm offering you, friend,' I added straightening on my hat and readying to leave, 'let's just say I give you fair warning.'

Then I left the same way I'd entered, Asa and my boys following me.

CHAPTER EIGHTEEN

You can bet I was watching my back on the way out of Wayne's house, or headquarters, or whatever you wanted to call it. No one had appeared out of nowhere, as I'd come to expect the men who hired on to the likes of Thad Wayne to do, but I still had a gut feeling that at least a handful of his men were close by. Besides, there was still that first thought that had struck me about the man, that he was a hideout-gun man. Oh, he didn't have the dress of a river-rat gambler, but I'd bet a year's wages that the man had been dealing from the bottom of a deck long before either of my boys were born, and that takes in quite a period of time.

I figured I had maybe ten or fifteen years on Wayne, which likely put him in the same age bracket as Ray Dunston. With that in mind, I also began to wonder if Dunston and Wayne might not have been partners once upon a time, they being the same age and all. Hell, it was even possible that they had come to Hogtown together, or at least at the same time. It wasn't out of the realm of possibility, and it wouldn't be the first time that an honest lawman had gone bad because the pay wasn't worth the risk. Not by a long shot.

I reckon you might say that was part of the reason I'd baited Thad Wayne the way I had. I knew that sooner or later us Carstons would wind up going up against Wayne and his bunch. And I knew that when we did, he'd need as much support as we could muster. Chance, of course, would figure that we were an invincible family, that all he needed was me and his brother beside him and a whole passel of those reloaded cylinders for those Colt .44s of his and we could take on the whole damned town if need be! Unfortunately, Chance tends to have more pride than a man should at times. Me, I knew that we'd have to have as many men and guns as possible. I knew I could count on Zeke Grant for support, although I wasn't that sure about the rest of the merchants in Hogtown, likely because I'd proven myself to Grant but not to them, individually. I was reasonably certain I could count on Davy Farnsworth, although he was also one I thought might have some difficulty, him being troubled by his father's death and all. I pictured Doc Grizzard as a healer more than a killer, and would be content to have him there when I got shot up rather than take a chance on getting killed alongside us. As for Jim Barnes, he seemed a whole lot more interested in getting the men he'd originally come to track down rather than help out the good folks of Hogtown.

But who's to say, he was there when we needed him earlier in the day, although he claimed to be after the man he'd shot and killed anyway. Maybe when he saw a fellow lawman in trouble, he'd come to his aid. Or maybe not. Still, that was a chance I'd have to take. My biggest concern at the moment was knowing whether or not I could trust Ray Dunston to take a hand in this game. The only thing I was sure of was that it wouldn't be long before I'd find out one way or another. Like I said, that's why I baited Thad Wayne the way I did.

Zeke Grant was doing business as usual when we walked into his store. I think he knew I had business with him of an official nature, for he took care of his customers in a quicker than usual manner. In the meantime, Asa took up his stance near the front door again, looking over the pots and pans he'd had such good luck with the day before, and Wash wandered through the store looking at this and that. Chance and me took to looking over some of the pistols and rifles Grant was keeping in stock.

'How good are you with these?' Chance asked, tossing a rifle to Zeke Grant. The man caught it at port arms, so he obviously knew at least the basics about firearms, like most men who'd served their country. Whether he was any good with the rifle was another question.

'I manage to keep fresh meat on the table,' was his reply, although he seemed a mite curious as to why Chance wanted to know his qualifications with a firearm.

It had been a long time since I'd done any storytelling, and now seemed like a good time to pick up on it.

'You know, Zeke,' I said, 'I knew a fella one time. Never had no trouble until one day a big, ugly, unlikable fella come into his backyard and said he wanted his land.

' "You can't have it," the landowner said. "It's mine."

' "Where'd you get it from?" the big ugly asked.

' "My father," the man said.

' "And where'd he get it?" big ugly asked.

' "From his father," the man said.

' "And where he get it?"

' "He fought for it." '

'The big ugly got a vicious look about him and said, "Well, I'll fight you for it." ' I paused a moment as the words sunk in.

'I don't see your point,' Zeke Grant said.

'My point, Zeke, is that most folks take a lot of things for granted until they have to fight for 'em. Until me and Asa Wilson and my boys come to town, old Thad Wayne figured he pretty well had the folks in Hogtown over a barrel.'

'True,' the store owner said in agreement.

'I just come from Thad Wayne's place,' I

198

said, cocking an eyebrow at the man. 'I all but told him I'd fight him for what he thinks is his in this town.'

'Pa also told him the townsfolk here wouldn't stand for a greedy man getting greedier,' Chance said.

'How's that?' Grant asked.

'The marshal here talked to my boys over in the hoosegow and found out it wasn't them that killed your bank teller, but some of Thad Wayne's yahoos,' Asa said in a determined way. 'What it comes down to is, Wayne and his men are not only bluffing you out of your monthly earnings, but robbing the town's bank as well.'

I could tell by the look about him that Zeke Grant had a fire building in him now, just like I was hoping he would. No one like Zeke Grant works as hard as he does for his money only to pass it over to the likes of Thad Wayne without so much as a fight. Damn it, money is just too hard to come by these days!

'We're only four men,' I said. 'If you want your town back, you and your fellow merchants are gonna have to lend a hand in getting it back.'

'We'd prefer you had a rifle or a pistol in that hand when you lend it too,' Chance added. That's Chance, always to the point.

'You won't get any argument from me on that,' Grant said, the rifle now firmly in his grasp. 'Just tell me what you want done.'

'I've got a notion my visit to Thad Wayne lit the fuse this morning,' I said.

'If I had one, I'd bet a dollar that keg of powder it's attached to is gonna explode today,' Chance added. 'I got the impression over the past couple of days that patience ain't Wayne's long suit.'

'What I'd like you to do, Zeke, is make the rounds of the rest of the merchants in town and tell 'em to get ready for some fireworks that ain't got nothing to do with the Fourth of July,' I said. 'Do you think they'll listen to you?'

By now Zeke Grant had grabbed a box of shells and was feeding them into the Henry rifle in his hand. Without taking his attention from loading the rifle, he said, 'If they want to keep their goddamn stores they will.'

'Good,' I said with a friendly smile, feeling good about enlisting the aid of one of the men I knew I could count on.

When he was finished loading his Henry, Grant looked up at me as he shoved the rest of the box of shells in an oversized pocket on his apron, which he still wore. 'You don't know how good it feels to be acting like a man again.'

'Even if there's the possibility of dying?' Chance asked.

'Mister,' Grant said, a firm, hard look to him, 'at least if I die, it'll be on my feet and not on my knees.'

'Good man,' Asa said with a wink. 'We'll close this operation down yet.'

'Damn sure betcha!' Grant said, and closed and locked his cash box.

I was about to give him a bit of a speech about how great he was doing, but knew it would be too long. But the man had enough fire in him to carry him through this battle, and needed little if any more prodding. Besides, I didn't get the chance anyway.

The ball opened right then and there.

A gunshot rang out from the marshal's office across the street, and I knew that Thad Wayne had made his move.

'Best be quick about getting hold of those merchants, Zeke,' I said on my way out of his store. 'I think that powder keg just went off.'

Indeed it had. As I crossed the street, I heard more gunfire coming from the jail. I was so excited about getting to the jail to find out whether I could count Ray Dunston as one of our own that I nearly didn't see the horse and rider that shot out of the alley next to the jail. He tossed a shot our way, not hitting anyone that I could see, and I immediately brought the Remington in my hand up to shoot back at him. I needn't have. I couldn't see who it was on the far side of the shooter's horse until the horse had sped away, but I reckon I should have expected it. Standing there, as cool as he could be, was Jim Barnes, a smoking gun in his fist as he looked down at the dead man lying in the dust of the street.

It only took one look to see that Ray Dunston was on our side, once I walked into the jail. He was sitting right behind his desk and had taken a gunshot wound to the chest before killing the man who lay in front of his desk. You could barely see for all the gun smoke in the place, but I managed to make out Tom and Jeremiah standing in their cells, each also holding a smoking pistol in his hand. They were the same handguns that Chance and I had slid to them when we'd visited them earlier. Like I said, they felt real secure by the time we left that jail. It's a good thing too, for if we hadn't left those guns with them, I had a notion they'd be laying there dead about now. Instead, they were able to fend off that yahoo in the alley who, I suspicioned, potshot them, not to mention the second of Wayne's men, who'd come through the front door of the jail.

Asa ran right past the men sprawled on the floor, wanting to know that his own boys were in good health. Seeing them standing upright like that did a world of good for the way the man was feeling, I think.

'Wash, get Doc,' I said, once I'd seen that Ray Dunston was still breathing, although semiconscious.

'You bet, Pa,' Wash said, and was gone pronto. He had a lighter frame than his older brother and I, so I knew he'd get to Doc's office quicker and safer than any of the rest of us. Besides, even if Thad Wayne's men were setting us up for an ambush, Wash could take care of himself. Hell, he'd survived four years of war, hadn't he? And he'd fought on the losing side, unlike his brother.

'Get another one of your horse thieves?' Chance asked Jim Barnes as he walked into the marshal's office in silence. 'Or was you just practicing your sharpshooting and needed a handy target?'

'You know, friend, you could really get on my nerves,' Barnes said as he pushed his hat back on his head. I'd never seen anyone like him, cool as could be when the lead started flying, hardly ever getting shot, and devil-may-care as you please about the whole affair.

'Now, children, this ain't the place for this kind of bickering,' I said in a half-serious voice. One thing about being my age is that you can always look at these younger men and call them children, no matter how grown-up they think they are. Especially when they happen to be acting like children and you both know it. Both Chance and Barnes knew it and were suddenly quiet.

'They come busting in,' Ray Dunston said

in a weak voice. He was losing blood, even with my neckerchief stuck over the wound, but he was a tough one who could endure pain. 'I've been expecting something like this,' he added, 'or I wouldn't have had my gun on the desk. Would've been dead by now.'

'I reckon being good's got something to do with staying alive in this profession,' I said, and promptly shut up as Doc Grizzard entered and shooed me away, immediately taking command of the situation.

From what I'd been able to make out before Doc arrived, these two yahoos had come charging in and caught Dunston off guard, but only one had gotten a shot off that hit the marshal before he killed the man. The Wilson boys had picked up where the marshal had left off once he'd been hit, Jeremiah keeping a gun on the cell windows as Tom did in the second man who had come charging into the marshal's office. Jeremiah had thrown a couple of shots at the man in the alley who had tried to potshot them, apparently scaring him enough to make him want to get away real quick. All he'd gotten away to was a quick death at the guns of Jim Barnes.

'I think it's about time we let you boys out of there,' I said, taking the keys on Ray Dunston's desk and unlocking the Wilson boys' cells.

'Thanks, marshal,' Tom said.

'Oh, he ain't concerned about whether or not you're innocent, boys,' Chance said with the sly grin of his.

'What?' I said, not believing my ears, for my oldest boy knew the law and how I felt about it better than that.

But Chance was still grinning, only ear to ear now. 'All Pa really wants to do, boys, is get your daddy off his back,' he said. Tom and Jeremiah laughed—hell, I even laughed after a minute or two—while Asa Wilson turned redder than a beet.

I'd just exchanged our guns for the Wilson boys' own firearms when Geraldine came flying through the door, a disastrous look about her and totally out of breath.

'Oh, marshal, it's merciful bad,' she managed to get out while trying to recover from whatever it was that had caused her to run like the wind.

'Wait a minute, ma'am, just slow down,' I said. 'Catch your breath and get it all out, Geraldine.' Chance handed over a cup of coffee, and I passed it on to the woman before me. 'Take a drink.' She did just that, made a sour face, but took some more until her dry throat was able to get the words out right. 'Now then, what's so urgent, missy?'

'Why, it's Thad Wayne, of course! He's gotten his whole crowd together and told 'em to hunt you all down. Why, you'd think he was that Santy Ana fella sounding the *deugello*, the call for no quarter,' she said, once again out of breath from spitting out the words so fast. Not that she'd told me anything I didn't already know. This was Thad Wayne's way.

'What else?' I asked. The rest in the office had suddenly gathered around Geraldine and me. All except for Doc and Ray Dunston, although I was sure both would hear the old woman.

'He don't like you disturbing his town, marshal. No sir.' Then she turned her attention to Jim Barnes. 'And he's got designs on you too, sonny.'

'Is that so?' Jim Barnes didn't seem flustered at all.

'Yes, that's so. Thad Wayne ain't too keen on his men being killed outright either, you know. I was you, sonny, I'd get out of town or get ready for a fight.'

'I ain't a runner and I ain't a quitter, ma'am,' Barnes said.

'One of his men said he knowed you,' she added.

'I'll bet it was the fella out in the street, wasn't it?' Barnes said, already knowing what the answer would be.

'Why, yes, yes it was.'

'And what name did he give Thad Wayne?' Barnes asked.

'Hickok,' she said, 'Wild Bill Hickok.'

'That's a fact, ma'am,' Barnes, or Hickok, confirmed.

CHAPTER NINETEEN

My mind was suddenly filled with things that had to be done and the all too perceptive knowledge that there wasn't enough time to get them done. Doc Grizzard and the men in the cells had surprised looks on their faces, likely about the real name of Jim Barnes. Maybe I'm getting old. Chance and Wash seemed to have heard of him and were glad he was there to assist us. Me, I'd never heard of the man. But then these so-called gunfighters were a new breed to me.

I quickly let the other two lawmen in the room, Dunston and Hickok, in on what I had Zeke Grant doing, so they wouldn't feel put upon if a good deal of the town merchants suddenly took up firing positions from the storefronts. Both Ray Dunston and Jim Hickok thought it a good idea and said so.

'We need to do one other thing,' Hickok added, and headed for the front door to the marshal's office.

'There's a whole lot we need to do,' I said, 'but what is it you've got in mind, young man?'

Hickok let out a whistle and pointed to someone across the street. In a matter of seconds a young boy of ten was standing before him. The lawman fished in his pocket for a dollar and planted it in the boy's hand.

'I've got an errand that needs to be done, and pronto.'

'Name it, mister. For this kind of money, I'll do just about anything you ask,' the boy said with a smile.

'You know most of the houses of the families that live here, do you?'

'You bet.' The boy sounded enthusiastic, but then for that kind of money, he likely should be.

'Good.' Then, glancing back and forth between the boy and me, he said, 'Most of the men are at work this time of day. It's likely that the women and young'uns are all at home. Son, I want you to run lickety split to each house and tell the woman of the house that there's gonna be a fearsome fight and to lock their houses up and get hold of a weapon of some kind. They're not to let anyone in, especially Thad Wayne's men. No one except a lawman.'

'Got it, sir.' The boy turned to leave, but Hickok grabbed hold of his arm, held him steady.

'You stay away from Thad Wayne's place and any of his men you see, understand?'

'Believe me, mister, I ain't stupid.'

Hickok smiled. 'No, I reckon not.'

Then the boy was gone.

'Good thinking, Hickok,' I said with a nod.

'If you don't plan on shooting at me, you can call me Jim.'

'Fine.' Then my mind was racing again and I started giving orders like a lawman's supposed to. 'Asa, I want you to stay here with Doc and—'

'Not hardly!' Somehow he must have known I was planning on leaving the lawman's office. Or maybe he'd figured I was just trying to get rid of him again so I wouldn't have to worry about him. 'You step foot out of this place and I'm gonna be with you and your boys. Tom and Jeremiah too.'

'Now, just hold on a minute, friend,' Doc Grizzard interrupted. 'I'm staying here because I've still got to tend to Ray's wounds. This medicating business takes a bit of time, you know. But if all of you leave, I'm gonna be stuck here with these killers,' he added, pointing a finger at the handful of Thad Wayne's men now behind bars. 'Hell, I'm no lawman, I'm a doctor!' His eyes squinted up as though by force of habit they made such a move whenever he got excitable. 'If your friends trust you enough to stay here to look after me and the marshal, I'd sure appreciate it. Asa, is that it?'

'Well,' Asa said, dragging the word out. 'If

that's how it is …' I do believe if there had been dirt on the ground, Asa would have kicked at it, but as it was, he scuffed his boot against the corner of the marshal's desk.

'That's how it is, Asa,' I assured him. 'What the Doc says is exactly what I've got in mind.'

'All right,' he stubbornly agreed. He didn't seem interested in what the rest of us might be doing at all, instead pulling a couple of rifles and a shotgun off the rifle rack and checking their loads. Asa was going to do just fine protecting Doc and Ray Dunston.

'If you boys want to come with me,' Hickok said to Tom and Jeremiah, 'we can keep an eye on these streets. I expect that Thad Wayne's bunch are gonna be coming momentarily.' He concluded by asking me, 'What about you, marshal?'

'I think Wash, Chance and I will head on down to the livery at the outskirts of town,' I said. 'We might be able to do some good there.'

'How's that?' Doc asked. For a man who was busy doctoring, he sure did seem curious about the goings-on around him. Why, if I didn't know better, I'd say he'd been taking lessons from Geraldine.

'Begging your pardon, Doc, but some of our generals did their best work with flanking movements and attacking from the rear,' Wash said with a good deal of pride.

210

'Oh, I see.'

'If Wayne and his men get you fellas surrounded like some Comanche war party on the raid, we can thin 'em out for you,' I said, picking up on my youngest's line of thought. Ever since my boys had come back from the war, they had slowly been letting out bits and pieces about where they'd been and what they'd done. I reckon it was their individual ways of letting anyone who was curious about it know what they'd done in that confounded conflict.

'You make sure and keep an eye on those prisoners, Asa,' I said before me and the boys left. 'They may be behind bars, but they ain't harmless by a long shot.'

I thought I saw a spark in my old friend's eye as he said, 'Yeah. I near forgot about that.' By the time I was out the door, that look in Asa Wilson's eye had turned devilish mean. And with a notion like that on his mind, I wasn't even going to ask the man what he had in mind. I just knew it was going to be a real hair raiser!

'I didn't know you were all that aware of General Lee's tactics, Pa,' Wash said when we were out on the street and heading for the Farnsworth Livery.

'Ain't you forgetting I spent a good many years fighting Indians and rangering, son?' I said with a disappointing frown.

'I hope you don't think those generals of

211

yours were the only ones who used flanking movements,' Chance said with what can best be described as a competitive glance. Once these boys got to discussing the war, they took bragging rights on each side as a serious matter.

'I got news for both of you,' I said before they could get started on a burning discussion on tactics. 'I learned more about flanking movements than any good dozen of your generals ever did at that fancy West Point school. Learned it from the Comanch' out here and the Blackfoot up in the Shinin' Mountains, by God!' That shut both of them up. 'Besides, I'm more interested in Davy Farnsworth's welfare at the moment than I am any game of tactics.' That buttoned the lips on both of my youngsters while we made the rest of our way to the livery in relative silence.

Thad Wayne was supposed to have twenty or so of these men who did his dirty work for him. I did some mental counting and figured up what we'd done in the way of either putting away or running off some of these hombres. Between Jim Hickok and us Carstons, I decided that we had gotten rid of about half of his men in one fashion or another. That left upwards of ten to deal with now that a showdown was near, unless of course he had some more tucked away in the woodwork somewhere. And if Thad

Wayne was a hideout-gun type, I wouldn't be surprised one bit that he had some extras to call on if things got tough for him. No sir.

Davy Farnsworth was nowhere in sight when we reached the livery, and I found myself unconsciously undoing the thong on the hammer of my holstered Remington. Something wasn't right.

'Davy!' I called, but got no answer.

At least not from Davy.

'He ain't here,' was the answer I got.

One thing about walking into a dark room like a saloon, or a livery, is that when the sun's out and in your eyes, you tend to take a minute or so to adjust your eyes right. So I hadn't seen the two men who stepped out from behind a stall and now had their guns trained on us. Like I said, something wasn't right, and I'd just discovered what it was.

'We been looking for him too, and he ain't here,' the second man said as the two moved forward a mite. I was sure they were part of Thad Wayne's outfit, although I couldn't recognize them right off.

'What do you want with the boy?' I asked, trying to play for more time and think of how we were going to get out of this fix all at the same time.

'Mr Wayne wanted to make an example of him to the town,' the heavyset gunman said, almost as though he were bragging about it. 'Killed his daddy, figured on doing the same thing to his troublemaking boy.'

My boys were standing next to me, both on my left side, which put me on the right and not far from the stalls on the right side of the livery.

'Too bad you lowdowns ain't got the guts to pick on a man of your own size,' Chance said, ready to pick a fight with either or both of the men. That was my boy, ready to take on the whole damned town.

I didn't know whether Chance had picked up on what I saw or was going to jaw this man to death, but I suddenly found myself glad that he'd taken over the talking, for I thought I'd seen a way out of this predicament. Fact of the matter was, I'd nearly forgotten about Otis and how precious a commodity he was. But there he was in his stall, still healthy and standing. He was also maybe five feet from the gunman to my front.

'Say, mister, you don't mind if I get rid of some wad, do you?' I asked real polite like, 'Gonna gag ary I don't spit here.'

'Long as you keep it away from me.'

'You bet.' I took a deep breath, gathered up the spit in my mouth and let fly a tolerable sling of the stuff. I made sure the gunman in front of me saw that I wasn't aiming at him either. But I hit my mark all the same.

I hit Otis square on the ass!

Now, hoss, there's lots of things you want to be careful about in life, and one of them is staying away from the ass end of an animal like Otis. Old Otis, he takes his backside kind of personal like, just like us humans. So you want to give him a wide berth when you walk around that side of him, for his leg has got a good reach, especially if he's in the kicking mood. And when his ass gets spit on as hard as I just did, why, old Otis gets in a kicking mood.

He likely didn't know who was behind him, and could have cared less, but his feet shot out at that gunman sharp and hard, kicking him square in the upper arm. Aside from doing considerable damage to the gunman, he also forced the man right into the side of his partner, knocking both men to the ground.

It was enough of a diversion for me and my boys to do some moving our own selves. Chance jumped on the gunman nearest me, while I tried to keep track of where his pistol went when it fell to the ground.

Wash had jumped on the other gunman, who still had a grip on his pistol, and the two of them had taken to rolling about in the hay. The man was a good deal bigger than Wash, and now had him on his back on the floor, swiftly bringing his gun hand around. I saw him bringing his pistol around to Wash's head. I barely had the loose pistol in my grip, knew in the back of my mind that I'd never make it in time to save my boy's life. Panic seized me as one thought raced through my mind!

He's gonna kill Wash!

A shot rang out from above me, and the man atop Wash slumped down on top of my boy in a lifeless hulk as a red spot began to form on his back, where a bullet had entered. I was bringing the gun in my hand up to the location of the sound, but when I saw who and where it had come from, I stopped.

'I ain't never shot a man in the back before,' young Davy Farnsworth said, looking down from the hay loft where he'd apparently been hiding from these men.

'Believe me, son, I don't care how you kill a rattlesnake,' I said, 'especially a sidewinder like this one.'

'These two would've done the same thing to us,' Chance said, now looking up at the boy in the loft. The man he'd tackled didn't appear to be dead, but he wasn't moving that much either, that I could see. 'You're forgetting what I told you, Davy, we're playing by their rules now.'

A look of terror came to the boy's eyes, but for the life of me, I couldn't understand why. How could Chance's words have terrified the boy so? How could—

'Look out, Chance!' he yelled, bringing his pistol up to shoot just as quick as the words were out. The bullet missed my oldest boy by inches, but hit its mark. When I saw him, the man Chance had been tangling with had another gun—likely a hideout gun of sorts—in his hand. If he'd gotten any further in his movements, Chance would have been dead. It was obvious in the manner in which he lay that the man would have backshot Chance.

'I think you just proved your case, Chance,' I said, and noticed that my oldest was wiping a hand across his forehead and collecting just as much sweat on his sleeve as I had.

'Well now, Davy, you're just full of life-saving deeds today,' Wash said with a grateful smile. I reckon that's one thing about my boys. They fight one another like the brothers they are, but I've never once seen them glad the other got hurt. Maybe that's what makes them the kind of brothers they are. Close.

Davy jumped down from the hay loft with little effort, landing solidly on his feet. Once down, he didn't try to examine the men he'd killed, like some men will. I thought I saw a look of shame and downright hurt on his face. That I could understand, for he was finding out that being mad enough to kill and actually doing the killing are two whole different canyons. Yes sir.

'I wonder if they have families?' the boy

said, a sad look about him now.

'If they do, they ain't gonna be missed,' Chance said.

'Yeah, Davy,' Wash added. 'If they got families, well, these are the kind of men who left 'em long ago and likely never cared for 'em anyways.'

'But how could you know that?' Davy asked, puzzled. I reckon he didn't figure Wash for knowing all that much, him being the youngest of the Carston Clan, even if he was more than a decade older than his own self.

'What you just experienced, Davy, is what we run into during that war we fought,' Wash said, a serious look about him now that old memories had been conjured up. 'And it sure ain't a pretty sight.'

'My brother's right,' Chance said. Ever since I could remember, Chance was always trying to have the last word on anything his younger brother spoke about. This time I was glad. 'Hell, we seen ten, no, a hundred times this many shootings, maybe more. Believe me, nothing gets easy about taking a man's life, even slimy bastards like these.'

'You just remember that you were on the side of the law, and maybe someday it'll make more sense to you, Davy,' I said.

I don't know what it was we said, but something had taken hold of the boy and somehow bolstered him, for he stuck the gun

218

in his waistband as though nothing had happened and gave me a businesslike look.

'Where're we going next?' All of a sudden he'd included himself in our group, sounding almost as persistent as Asa Wilson.

'Well, don't you want to stay here and protect your livery, son?' I asked. Now the boy truly did have me confused. 'After all, it was your daddy's, wasn't it?'

'They can burn it to the ground if they want,' the boy said in what I took to be a hard voice. 'It don't mean a helluva lot anymore, not without Pa. All I want is—'

'I know, son,' I said, knowing exactly what his next words were going to be.

'Thad Wayne,' Chance said.

'Yeah,' Davy said with a nod.

When we left, the livery was locked up, but the two would-be killers were slumped against the front doors of the livery stable. On the chest of one I'd tacked a note that read: ALL TRESPASSERS WILL BE DEALT WITH IN THIS MANNER.

The four of us had just finished reloading our pistols when we heard sporadic gunfire coming from the middle of town.

CHAPTER TWENTY

We began working our way back toward the jail. The spooky thing was that although we could hear a lot of gunfire, there didn't seem to be anybody out on the streets.

'I reckon facing a man in the open hasn't proven too fruitful for Thad Wayne's boys,' I said as we proceeded with caution.

'That's gunfire coming from the rear of those buildings,' Davy Farnsworth said, gun in hand.

'Just what I was thinking,' Chance said with a nod.

'You got a good head on your shoulders, Davy,' Wash added, which made the boy blush some, even though, as I suspicioned, there was a good deal of pride in what showed on his face. I found myself feeling glad we'd brought Davy Farnsworth along. He was really proving out.

The gunfire was suddenly nearer, in a store next to Zeke Grant's, which according to the sign was a laundry business run by a Chinaman. They must have broken in through the back entrance and were now in the store searching out inhabitants. One last final shot was heard, and the Chinaman, likely the owner, came flying through the plate-glass window, his midsection falling on the jagged broken glass still set in the frame. But I doubted he felt it, for the way his body slumped there, it was obvious that the man was dead long before the glass cut him to pieces.

Chance tossed a piece of lead at a corner of glass that hadn't shattered yet, sending tiny fragments flying every which way inside the laundry. Either it scared the invaders or they had finished the business they had come for and were leaving anyway, for they offered no return fire when the four of us ran across the street.

About halfway across the street it seemed like we were safe, for there didn't seem to be any firing at all. Then, almost to the other side of the street, a bunch of dust began kicking up at our heels, and I felt some splinters of wood fly past my face. It was Davy and me who were following Chance and Wash, so we both stopped at the same time, right out there with little or no shelter, and each let fly a shot at what turned out to be our two potshotters. I had the distinct feeling that, as we both turned to fire, young Davy was thinking the same way I was. Like me, he must have heard the shots coming from the roof in back of us, and hitting these pilgrims was no problem, for they were standing bold as brass when we turned. We each shot one about the middle of the chest, and these hombres soon dropped their rifles and slumped over the backboard they once hid behind, dead as a horse apple from old Otis.

Davy didn't say a thing, just gave me a quick nod and made a hasty exit to the boardwalk we were originally heading for. He didn't seem shaken either, not like he had been earlier over the man he'd killed. I reckon he was finding out that getting shot at in earnest will do something to your system that just bypasses the portion of your brain that recognizes fear. I didn't know about young Davy Farnsworth, but I'd always found that getting shot at made me madder than hell, which added a good deal of determination to making sure that it didn't happen to me again any time soon. 'Good shooting, son,' Chance said, knocking on Zeke Grant's general store at the same time he spoke. 'Open up, Zeke, it's the Carstons! We come to help.'

The sound of a lock being undone was quick in the coming, as Zeke hurried to let us in.

'Davy, I want you and Wash to watch the side alleys, while Chance and me help out Mr Grant,' I said before the doors to the store opened to let us in.

'You bet,' was all the boy said, knowing that Wash had heard my order. In a matter of seconds the boys were covering the alleyways of the store.

222

Two of Thad Wayne's men were coming through the back entrance to Zeke's store as we walked in. He must have figured it was the rudest thing that ever happened to him, but pushing him hard as he could was the only thing Chance could do to keep Zeke Grant from getting backshot. Me, I hit the first one high in the chest, sending him crashing back into the rifle rack he was right in front of, while his partner snapped a shot at me that took my John B. off my head and had me ducking to the floor too. If trading shots was what this fellow wanted, then I'd oblige him, and after two more shots and some broken plate-glass, he retreated out the back. But he had a surprise waiting for him if he thought he was going to get clean away from us. I heard another pistol shot fired outside and took it to be Davy, who had covered this side of the alley.

Cautiously, I made my way back through the back entryway while Chance was profusely apologizing to Zeke Grant and helping him up off the floor. Just outside the back door lay the man I'd just finished trading shots with. He still had his gun in hand, but he was never going to use it again, not if the lifelessness of his body was any indication.

'You keep shooting this good, maybe you ought to run for lawman in this town,' I heard Wash say at the other end of the alley,

223

then looked up the alley to see him patting the boy on the back as he spoke.

'Let's make sure we get out of this scrape alive before we start telling one another how great we are,' I said, half in a growl, half in jest, as I moved back inside.

'Looks like a good place to do some reloading,' Chance said back inside.

'Yeah,' Wash agreed as he entered the store with Davy. 'At least we got the fixings. Only trouble is, I ain't needing the reloading.' I didn't recall Wash firing any shots so far.

'Then you watch the door,' I said, while Chance, Davy, and I tended to our six-guns for about ten minutes. If you're experienced in these matters, it doesn't take but a minute to get a good reload taken care of. Hell, the only choice you've got on these plains is learning how to be quick or die, if you think about it.

'You gonna be able to keep an eye on this fella?' I asked Zeke Grant when I was finished reloading.

'You bet. Just strip him of his weapons and maybe keep him from dying on the spot, but don't you worry, he'll be live enough to hang when this mess is over. I'm gonna bolt and lock that back door too. Give me a mite more ease in fighting off this bunch.'

'Good.'

'Say, marshal,' Grant said before we left.

224

'Do you think you've got anyone who could stay and help me out? I'm no gunman, and if they're operating in pairs, I could sure use the help of someone to even the odds.'

'Davy, what do you think about staying with Mr Grant and helping him out?' I asked the boy, talking to him like he was one of my deputies, which in a way I reckon he was. 'I never sent a man to do something I wasn't capable of doing my own self, son, but I also figure that if a man signs on for the fight, why, he oughtta follow orders too. What do you think?'

'Anything you say, marshal,' was the boy's reply.

'*Will*, Davy. The men I know who call me friend also call me Will,' I said with a wink and a nod. Chance and Wash were watching the two of us, and I think they knew as well as I that my words had meant a hell of a lot to Davy Farnsworth. But then the first time a boy who's been reminded that he's between hay and grass gets called a man, well, that means a lot. A whole lot.

'You bet, Will.'

I wanted to tell Davy how much it had meant to me when that first happened, when I'd first been called a man way back when. But today seemed to be one of those days when all you wind up doing is putting out fires here and there.

A gunshot rang out across the street, and I

thought it sounded like it might have come from the jail. But like I say, I'm getting old.

I reckon Zeke Grant knew that us Carstons had to be going mighty quick, for he said, 'Don't you worry about Davy here. We've always gotten along real fine. Things get tough, we'll help you out ary we can.'

'I know you will,' was all I had time to say before I raced out the door, following my boys toward the marshal's office.

Asa Wilson's boys and Jim Hickok were running toward the jail too. They must have heard the shots and figured someone had tried to do in Asa again. And maybe they were right, for Asa and the marshal should have been the only ones who had six-guns in that place.

I thought I heard another horse gallop away from the side alley of the jail and toward the rear. We entered the jail with guns drawn, rather than out into the street, as had happened once before.

CHAPTER TWENTY-ONE

The shooting had come from the inside of the jail, all right. From all of the gun smoke inside the marshal's office, it looked like at least three or four shots had been fired. Ray Dunston was still in the seat at his desk and looking all sorts of alert with his gun in hand. He still wasn't in any shape to go gunfighting, mind you, but I had a notion he'd do real well just from where he was sitting. Asa Wilson lay on the floor, blood spattered across the front of his chest, Doc Grizzard kneeling at his side. Geraldine stood in the corner, a scared look about her.

'Well, don't just stand there, damn it!' Doc commanded. 'One of you fools get over here and help me get Asa over to that cot.' Tom and Jeremiah were there in an instant, gently picking the man up as though he were nothing. Looking at Asa right then, he might not have been. He'd lost some weight before we'd come up to this Hogtown, not to mention losing a mite more on the trip to this hellhole. He was always rail thin, that I could remember, but looking at him being carried so effortlessly by his sons, why, I would have been surprised if the man weighed much more than a hundred ten pounds.

On the other hand, Asa Wilson turned out to be quite something, which said a lot for the man. Yes indeed. It was Ray Dunston who related to us the story of what had taken place.

'A couple of Wayne's men tried the same thing they'd done earlier,' he said in a weak voice. Still, I couldn't pry that pistol from his hand, not even with the reassurance that the shooting was over and that everything was all right now. 'I heard 'em throw a couple of pistols in through the cell window. Asa was in a better position to do anything about it than me, so he had his gun out, and shot at least two of 'em that I know of.' He paused here and stretched to look over his should to confirm what he said next. 'Yup, he killed that son of a bitch Faraday. Sure did.'

Chance took a long stride over to the cell and gave it a gander, then a low whistle of astonishment. 'Don't get much deader than this, Pa.'

I took a few steps and looked the scene over. Two of them were dead, all right. Asa had apparently put two slugs in one man and at least three that I could count in Faraday's chest. There was too much blood on them and on the floor around them for either of them to be alive.

'What about the other two?' I asked, noticing that the second pair of men looked sound asleep.

It must have hurt him to do so, but Ray Dunston gave a hearty chuckle anyway. 'Doc and your friend can sure be devious,' he said with a smile. 'Took my coffeepot and used the rest of the coffee to mix with some of Doc's laudanum. Those two were the only ones thirsty enough to drink the coffee. Put 'em out like a light, though.'

'That it surely did.' So that was the sly

look that Asa had about him when we'd left earlier. I should have known he'd think of something like this to cut down the odds.

'I don't know about you, Will,' Jim Hickok said, all business now, 'but it seems to me that this Wayne character had his men trying to occupy as many of these stores as he can.' It was the first time I'd heard him call me by my first name. Maybe there was hope for the man yet.

'I know just what you mean, Jim,' I replied, shaking my head in despair. 'They're a ruthless bunch too. See what they've done to that Chinaman across the street?'

'Yeah. Of course, I'm getting the notion that these merchants don't do much more fighting than with their wives.'

'For some of them, fighting with their wives is likely as much violence as they ever want to see,' Chance said with a sly grin.

'How do you shut him up?' Hickok asked me, serious as could be. It was easy to see that the man didn't like Chance's sense of humor any more than I did at times.

'What I do is give him something to work besides his mouth,' I said, mostly just to see how Chance would get out of this predicament. I swear there are times I really want to see that boy squirm.

'Fine. Why don't you come with me, Chance, and we'll see if you're as tough as some of those words you like to throw around,' Hickok said in a no-nonsense tone of voice.

'Oh? And just what is it you've got in mind?'

Jim Hickok glanced down at Chance's dual pistols, then at his own, and nodded agreement with whatever it was he was thinking. 'The way I figure it, if we don't waste any bullets, we should be able to put half of these hombres out of business right quick.'

'Now you're talking my kind of language,' Chance said with a smile that said he was going to enjoy this, no matter how much he didn't like being talked down to by this man.

'Good. Will,' Hickok said to me, 'I'm gonna borrow your son and see if the two of us can't scare some of these amateurs out of these merchant's stores. The plug-uglies don't belong there anyway.'

'Sounds good,' I said, although I have to admit that I was a good deal concerned over Chance's welfare. You know how it is when a couple of young squirts get together; no matter how serious the situation may get, the two of them are always competing, always trying to outdo the other like it was some kind of game they were playing. 'You boys just make sure you get back here alive, understand?'

'What's the matter, Pa? Worried?' Chance asked, still grinning.

He was close enough for me to reach out and grab a handful of his shirtfront, which is just what I did.

'Listen, sonny,' I said, breathing good and hard in his face now. 'I come here with the distinct intention of taking my whole family back to Twin Rifles with me. And I mean in an upright position. You got that?'

'Sure, Pa.' Chance eased his shirt out of my fist real slow and in as orderly a manner as you'd ever see him act. 'No reason to get riled.'

'You two just make sure you do your job, and stop trying to show off for one another,' I growled. 'Smart-aleck kids,' I muttered to myself as the two of them left by the back door.

'Looks like you and me are stuck with each other, Wash,' I said with a smile.

'That's fine with me, Pa. I wouldn't have it any other way.'

'You got some other plans, Will?' Ray Dunston asked. All of a sudden I was on a friendly first-name basis with just about everyone in the marshal's office.

'Well, what Jim Hickok said makes sense. Seems about right to help these merchants out as much as we can,' I said. 'What do you say, Wash? Think we can do as good a job as the two showoffs that just left?'

'Better, Pa,' Wash said, checking the loads on both his guns.

'I reckon you two will have enough on your hands looking after your pa,' I said to the Wilson brothers.

'We'll take care of looking out for Doc and Pa and the marshal there,' Tom said. 'Don't you worry. Will, ain't nobody coming through that door that's gonna live to tell about it if he ain't friendly about it.'

'I believe you, son.' And I did. Tom and Jeremiah were about as fed up with this town and the way it was run as us Carstons and Ray Dunston and the good doctor seemed to be. 'I got a notion we're gonna put a stop to these scoundrels today.'

'Marshal,' Geraldine said, suddenly grabbing my arm as Wash and I were heading for the back door of the jail.

'Yes, ma'am,' I said, surprised. I had nearly forgotten about her, in the busy action that had taken place so far today.

'Listen, marshal,' she said in a soft but firm voice. 'You make sure that *you* come back alive. I've taken to worrying over you Carstons, you know.'

You could have knocked me over with a feather! I'd gotten so used to giving orders that I'd long since given up on anyone saying much about how nice it would be to have my own old carcass coming back in one piece. As for Geraldine, well, she wasn't much to look at, but she knew how to give out some warmth when it counted, and I found myself greatly appreciating her words.

'Don't you ever doubt it, old girl,' I said with a smile. 'We'll have a drink over this whole mess yet.' Then I leaned down and kissed her gently on the cheek.

'Oh, marshal,' she said with a blush. 'Go on.' Yes sir, I was really taking a liking to her.

Wash and I took off in the opposite direction that Hickok and Chance had gone. It seemed awful quiet on the side of the street with Zeke Grant's store and the Chinaman's laundry on it. I got to wondering if Thad Wayne's men hadn't skipped some of those stores and taken up pestering some on this side of the street. Or had the merchants cut and run? Had they lost all desire to live in this town and decided to find another place to call home? All of which raised another question: Were all of us—Hickok and us Carstons—going through these merchants' stores for nothing? Were we laying our lives on the line for men who no longer cared? I certainly hoped not.

'You look worried, Pa,' Wash said as we neared the back entrance of a feed and grain store.

'It's nothing boy, nothing.'

'I sure hope so.'

We entered the back door of the store, taking our steps slowly so as not to be noticed by whoever was in the place, and there were definitely sounds in the store. There proved to be no one inside the back door in a storage area, so we made our way to the main business area. We stopped dead in our tracks when we got there.

There were three of them, and they had killing on their mind.

'I told you, mister, I want to know where your money is,' one of them said to the storekeeper.

'No,' the man said defiantly. 'I ain't telling you and you ain't getting it!' Wash must have thought I was crazy when he saw the grin on my face, but this man had just reaffirmed what I had doubted out there in the alley. By God, these folks were willing to die for what was theirs.

The tough-talking man with a gun cracked the barrel across the face of the proprietor, knocking him down. In a way, that was good, for it was then I decided that this was going to come to a quick, screeching halt. I shot the gun out of the man's hand, saw it go flying up in the air as he looked around to his rear.

'Drop it!' I yelled, cocking my Remington again. But the man's partners hadn't had enough, and pulled their guns around toward Wash and me.

I shot one while Wash shot the other, and both shots were true. These fellows would never rob another store. Their friend, the one whose gun I'd shot out of his fist to begin the ball, had suddenly disappeared, running out the front door and heading directly across the street to the saloon.

Wash and I checked the proprietor out. He'd have a sore jaw for a while and maybe some broken merchandise to replace, but he was still alive, and thankful for that.

I heard a rash of gunfire from one of the stores on the other side of the jail and knew in an instant that it was from the guns of Hickok and Chance. Then the gunfire sounded like it had quickly moved to the streets. I took a step outside, and sure enough, there were Chance and Jim Hickok, standing right out in the middle of the street like a couple of damn fools and trading lead with anyone who seemed foolish enough to shoot at them.

I rushed out in the street myself, Wash right behind me.

'Get off the goddamn streets!' I yelled at Chance and Hickok.

A shot whizzed past me and I heard a groan. Over my shoulder I saw Wash falling to the ground, felt my hand firmly grip my Remington, and tossed a shot in the direction I'd thought it had come from. I missed whoever he was, wherever he was. Suddenly I didn't care about the fight, didn't care about who was shooting at who. All I could see was my youngest boy laying there on the ground in the middle of the street of this godforsaken town. Damn it, he was bleeding!

He wasn't unconscious. In fact, he still had his gun in his hand, Wash did. But he sure did look laid out awful flat, and I didn't like that. Not one bit.

'Wash!' I said, quickly kneeling down beside him.

'I'm all right, Pa,' the boy said, although I thought he sounded faint. Or maybe it was just my hearing. After all, I'm getting old, and I don't mind telling you that right then it was telling on me a lot. I could feel the pain in the boy, had forgotten what was going on about me. Totally forgotten it all.

'Pa!' Chance yelled it out loud and clear. When I heard him, I also noticed that the gunfire had calmed down quite a bit. Then I looked behind me and knew why it was that the man I'd shot in the grain store had run toward the saloon.

Chance and Hickok were walking toward me, guns holstered. You'd think they were taking a simple stroll down the main street, they looked that calm about the whole thing. It was when I looked to my rear that I saw the seven or eight men who'd just come out of the saloon. I'd bet my life they were the reinforcements that man running into the saloon wanted. All armed and looking like they wanted to do some killing.

'Lawman, say your prayers,' the man who apparently served as the leader growled. I stood up to my full height and faced them. Like the man said, at least I'd die on my feet and not my knees.

'Got a bone to pick, do you?' I said.

I reckon this bird wanted to do all the talking, for he seemed to ignore me. 'Chuck,' he said to one of his men, 'take a couple of the boys and drag old Dunston and that doctor out of the jailhouse. They can die right alongside this old geezer.'

I frowned at the man as three of his men lit out for the marshal's office. Chance and Hickok had stopped beside me and were facing the crowd from the saloon. The fact that they outnumbered us by a good two to one didn't seem to faze either one of them. Me, I don't mind telling you I was getting a mite edgy about the whole situation.

Those three yahoos made no bones about kicking the door to the marshal's office wide open and rushing in, guns drawn. Just like you'd figure, there was a lot of shooting once they were in. But I had a notion that none of them would be coming back out on their feet. They'd likely have to be carried back out feet first, at least if Tom Wilson kept his word on how intruders would be treated within the four walls of Ray Dunston's office.

'They ain't coming back out, fellas, so let's

get down to business,' Hickok said in a serious tone. To the spokesman for this lot of toughs, he said, 'Warren, ain't that your name?'

'What's it to you?' Warren had suddenly gotten cautious and concerned about the lawman's nosy question.

'There's wants and warrants on you back in Missouri. I aim to take you back for a judge to talk to.' Jim Hickok was sounding more and more like a man of his word.

'You ain't taking me back noplace.'

'Oh, yes I am.' Hickok gave a short shrug of the shoulders. 'It's up to you how you go. It can be on your feet or facedown, don't much make a difference to me.'

'I said I ain't going,' Warren said with a near vehement tone to his voice.

I never had been one for a whole lot of talking when there were things to be done.

'Boys, I think the whole lot of you had better either fill your hand or shuck those guns,' I said, 'and I mean now.'

We were all going for our guns—me and Chance included—when young Hickok all but blinked and had both six-guns in his hands, firing one shot from each into Warren, who dropped like a wounded buffalo and never got off a shot.

'Smart-aleck kids,' I muttered aloud as I shot the youngster to my front, just to show them I wasn't that much of an old geezer. I only wounded him in the leg, and he still had a gun in his hand when he went down, was still willing to fight it out to the end. He would have gunned me down for sure if it weren't for Hickok, who quick as you please planted another slug in the man's heart, leaving him for buzzard meat.

Chance did a quick clean job of killing two more of the would-be gunmen, an action which proved what I'd suspected all along—they were all a bunch of amateurs when it came to this newfangled gunfighting profession. Chance proved he was just as good as any of them. Now all I had to hope was that my oldest boy wouldn't decide to take up this profession, lover of guns that he was.

What surprised me about the whole shootout was two things. The first was the shot that came from behind me, which came from Wash, who still had his own pistol firmly in his grasp. But he didn't shoot at any of the men before us. By the time I turned around to see where he was shooting, I heard the body of a dead man fall off the roof atop the saloon. If they weren't fast, at least Thad Wayne's men were proving to be devious sorts—almost as bad as their boss.

The second surprise came from the marshal's office.

'Sonny! You're wonderful!' It was Geraldine, who had made fast to get to

Wash. But those were the only two words I heard her speak, for Thad Wayne, the boss himself, had finally shown up and was about to play a hand in this game.

I don't know where he rightly came from, maybe the alleyway beside the marshal's office. I still don't know. All I know is that he was suddenly there and had a big arm around Geraldine, holding her firmly in front of him as a shield. His men were all gone now, so I reckon hiding behind a woman's skirts was all that was left for the likes of Thad Wayne.

'Drop your guns, all of you!' he commanded. When none of us moved, he added, 'I swear to God that if you don't, I'll kill her here and now.' He meant business just as much as Jim Hickok did, that much I could recognize in his voice, although I also thought I'd picked up a trace of fear. Even men like Thad Wayne sweat in a tight spot, and he was definitely in one now.

I didn't drop my gun. Neither did my boys or Jim Hickok. Oh, we holstered them all right, but that was the extent to which we went to putting them away.

'It's your move, Wayne,' I said in a hard voice. 'You just better know that you ain't gonna get out of this place. Not hardly.'

'We'll see about that,' he said, a touch more fear showing in him now. Maybe the truth of my words had gotten across to him.

That was when we all got a surprise.

Out of the door of the marshal's office, directly to Wayne's rear, staggered a half-dead Asa Wilson. Hatless, he had a chest full of blood that made his shirt hardly recognizable. But perhaps the important thing about the man was the six-gun in his fist and the determined look in his eye. Silently, he raised the gun until he had it at arm's length, aimed directly at the hulk of a man who was Thad Wayne.

'Drop it, you son of a bitch, or I'll kill you where you stand,' he said in a voice that was just as determined as the look in his eye.

Something hit Thad Wayne just then, and it was hard telling exactly what it was. The realization that I was right, that he wasn't going any place but to jail that day? The fear of dying? I couldn't tell. Hell, no one really wants to die. I know I don't. Do you? Of course not! But Thad Wayne had a look about him that was just as mystifying as Asa Wilson's was direct and to the point. I think Hickok or any one of us Carstons could have potshot the man right then without fear of harming Geraldine, but it was that damned uncertainty that the man gave off that had us all buffaloed at the moment. Only one thing was certain, and that was that the man's brain was turning, that somehow or other he was trying to beat the odds.

'All right, old man, you win,' Wayne said,

241

and holstered his own pistol.

'What the hell—' both Chance and Hickok started to say at once. But we all found out soon enough what it was the man was up to.

I said he was a hideout-gun man from the start! And by God he was! He palmed that two-shot derringer just as slick as an ace up his sleeve. Then he started using it. His first shot went to Asa Wilson, hitting him square in the chest and felling him easily, when you consider the amount of lead he was likely carrying around in him anyway. Then he stuck the palm gun right in Geraldine's stomach and used his second shot.

That tore it!

Hoss, where I come from it's bad enough when you hide behind a woman's skirts. But when you go to shooting them, why, you might as well call it quits, for you've just dig your own grave!

Chance and Hickok and I all had our guns out, all had them ready to use, would have killed the man on the spot. But we didn't. We all three stopped at having them out and in hand. I don't know why. Maybe it was some intimate knowledge that we would be entering upon a personal fight at that point. Maybe it was seeing Davy Farnsworth and Doc Grizzard come out with a weapon each in their hands.

Davy had that pistol of his and walked

right out of Grant's General Store, stopping on the boardwalk. I don't know whether he saw Asa Wilson make one last move when he brought that six-gun of his up and shot Thad Wayne in the side, but it was just after Asa's gun was fired that Davy aimed and fired his own, hitting Wayne high in the chest and spinning him around. He was cocking his pistol for a second shot, intent, I'm sure, on killing the man who had killed his father, but he needn't have.

Doc Grizzard had that sawed-off shotgun that Asa had pulled off the rack in Ray Dunston's office earlier in the day. Cocked and ready to fire, he waited until the big coward who thought he had once run this town turned to partially face him. Then Doc pulled a trigger and Thad Wayne took a load of buckshot in the upper stomach, bleeding all over himself as he fell to the ground.

'Worthless scum,' I heard Doc growl at the sight before him. For a man who was used to fixing people up, old Doc Grizzard had just done one hell of a lot of damage.

By the time he had finished growling his words, I had made my way over to Asa Wilson, who didn't have long left in this life, if he wasn't dead already. I rolled him over on his side, gently setting him down on his back. The entire boardwalk was covered with his blood.

'Old Doc ain't gonna be able to patch up

this hole,' I heard him say, although just barely.

'Here now, Asa,' Doc said, laying the shotgun down beside Asa and kneeling down by his side. A tear rolled down his cheek, and I knew it wasn't for the likes of Thad Wayne, 'You haven't even give me a chance.'

'Doc'll—' I started to say, but Asa grasped my sleeve and gave a hard tug.

'Don't go feeding me syrup now, Will,' he near sputtered, blood coming out of his mouth as he attempted to talk. 'I'm too bitter to take it, and you know I never took nothing but the truth.'

'Asa, shut up. The truth is we got the sonsa-bitches,' I said, a sadness welling up in me. 'That's the truth.'

Slowly he smiled, just the way I'd always remember him. 'Yeah,' he said. Then he slumped back, dead.

A crowd had gathered now that the shooting had stopped, and just like buzzards, they had gathered around the fresh meat, Thad Wayne and Asa Wilson. But a man ought to have some kind of dignity when he dies, and I never did picture people gawking at you like you were part of a circus as being anything close to dignified.

'What the hell you looking at?' I said when I was on my feet. 'Ain't nothing but a man who died to save your town. Hell, there's plenty of 'em around. Go look at your stores

244

and be thankful you've got men like that. They're likely the only ones who'll know peace today.'

'The man's right, folks,' Chance said. 'You've got your town back. Now start tending to it like it belonged to you.'

'He sure had a lot of guts,' Jim Hickok said, looking down at Asa Wilson. Hickok hadn't been hit, so I had second thoughts about whether a man who hadn't been shot in a fracas really had that much to say about it. On the other hand, I hadn't expected that from Hickok either.

Besides, he sure was good with those guns.

CHAPTER TWENTY-TWO

I got lucky that day. The only thing that got aerated was my John B., and I was grateful for that.

As for Thad Wayne, I do believe the townspeople would have shoveled some dirt right over where he lay and be done with the man and his ways. They had that much hate for the outlaw. But I reckon all that learning they'd gotten in their youth took over someplace and they'd wind up burying him in boot hill.

We all owed a lot to Asa Wilson for taking a hand in saving our lives and giving his own.

Tom and Jeremiah, who had indeed done in those three yahoos who'd made the mistake of storming into the marshal's office, got real upset when Doc Grizzard made a passing comment about burying their father in boot hill. I reckon the Wilson brothers were as lucky as me in this fracas, for neither had come away with so much as a scratch.

'You just show us where we can buy a buckboard, and we'll be taking Pa for a proper burial back to Twin Rifles and the ranch he worked,' Tom had told Doc. Davy Farnsworth would have given Tom and Jeremiah the buckboard for free, but the town pitched in and purchased one for them to take their father back to his home. Fact of the matter is that young Jim Hickok even managed to finagle a buckboard for the two men he'd come after, who were no longer in the standing position.

Either Ray Dunston wasn't as bad off as he originally looked or he was tougher than I'd given him credit for, because the next day, when we'd readied to leave, I made a point of stopping by his office to see who was going to sit in for him while he was recovering.

'Well, I'll be,' was all I could think to say when I sauntered into his office. Oh, he had his arm in a sling, all right, and a shirt draped loosely over his left shoulder, but he didn't look any the worse for wear. Why, he even had his six-gun strapped on.

'Looks like you underestimated the man, Pa,' Chance said to my rear.

'I reckon I did, son,' I said in about as apologetic a manner as I'd ever get. I never was big on making up for my mistakes, but then few men are. Still, there are times it calls for a few straightforward words, and this was one of them. I glanced at Davy Farnsworth, who sat at a table in the corner, cleaning his pistol. You'd think it had become a part of his anatomy, the way he was paying close attention to it. (He was another one who'd come away from the fight relatively unscathed, with only a flesh wound in the arm.) 'You know, son, you could do worse than to look to this man for some guidance once in a while,' I said to Davy. 'Don't never take him for granted either.'

'Zeke Grant was in earlier this morning,' Ray Dunston said. 'To hear him talk, I ought to make Davy my deputy. Done some fine shooting yesterday, from what Zeke says.'

'That's a fact, Ray,' I said with a nod.

'Couldn't do much better,' Wash said from the doorway, his own arm in a sling. 'Man saved my life yesterday, and I'm grateful for that.'

'I know,' Ray said, then, glancing at Davy added, 'we been talking about that.'

I shook his hand and wished him well. He, in return, promised me that the men in his jail wouldn't be leaving except to attend a trial, and most likely, a hanging. I told him I knew they would.

I was getting ready to mount up outside when Davy made his way out to the boardwalk.

'I wanted to say good-bye the proper way to you, Will,' he said, and offered a hand. I took it and knew from his firm grip that I'd made a friend for life in Davy Farnsworth during my stay in Hogtown.

'You've done a lot of growing the last couple of days, son,' I said, standing back and taking in the lad's features.

'Been a lot happening.' He was silent awhile, the kind of awkward silence that comes between two people who are about to say good-bye but don't really want to. 'The marshal says things are changing. Do you think so?'

'Son, as old as I am, I try not to ponder that subject too awful much,' I said in reply.

Chance laughed. 'Things are always changing, kid. Every day.'

'You just got to remember one thing, Davy,' Wash said. 'The more things change, the more they stay the same.'

Davy Farnsworth had a puzzled look on his face as he said, 'I'll have to think on that one.'

'You do that son,' I said as I mounted and wheeled my horse toward the direction we'd entered Hogtown. 'Someday it'll make a lot of sense to you. Guaranteed.'

I left the boy with that bit of advice, knowing that someday he'd see the truth in all of it. Age does that to you.

We rode out of Hogtown that day, the Wilsons and us Carstons, and started our trek back to Twin Rifles.

'Oughtta be an easier ride going back then it was coming,' Chance said outside of town.

'I sure hope so, son,' I said.

'What are you worried about, Pa?' Wash said, puzzled.

I looked back at our pack mule.

'Son, if we don't get Otis there back in prime shape, why, Old Man Farley's gonna make that fracas at Hogtown look like child's play when he hunts us down.'

All of sudden Chance and Wash looked about as worried as I was feeling.

But then that's the way of it, ain't it? One damn thing after another.